Books by Graham Reed

The Chairman's Toys

The Chairman's Toys

Graham Reed

Poisoned Pen Press

First Edition 2018

10 9 8 7 6 5 4 3 2 1

Library of Congress Control Number: 2018930049

ISBN: 9781464211089   Hardcover
ISBN: 9781464210075   Ebook

Poisoned Pen Press
4014 N. Goldwater Blvd., #201
Scottsdale, AZ 85251
www.poisonedpenpress.com
info@poisonedpenpress.com

Printed in the United States of America

For Val

Chapter One

I was just starting to enjoy the party when The Norwegian came out of the bathroom and ruined everything.

At the time, I was dancing with a hyperkinetic yoga enthusiast named Windy. Or possibly Mindy. All attempts at verbal communication were being swallowed up by the blizzard of techno coming out of the forty-thousand-dollar stereo system. Which was fine by me since I didn't imagine Windy-Mindy and I had all that much to talk about anyway.

She looked about a decade younger than me—clocking in somewhere south of thirty—and it was manifestly evident that her lifestyle choices were largely antagonistic to my own. Shrink-wrapped in Lululemon, Windy-Mindy radiated health and vigor as she bounced around in fuchsia Nikes performing an ode to the benefits of healthy living expressed through the medium of interpretive dance.

Exhausted by the spectacle, I took a breather and another belt of Woodford Reserve. In an attempt to bridge the cultural divide, I waggled the bottle at Windy-Mindy, inquiring with my eyebrows. Her brow furrowed but the corners of her mouth did curl up slightly—one patronizing, the other amused. Or so the bourbon whispered to me.

It may have been correct because she countered by proffering her own bottle—the blue-tinted plastic kind that hikers and college students liked to clip to their backpacks. In her other hand were two small white tablets, which I lip-read to be Vitamin C.

I shrugged and swallowed.

The contents of the bottle turned out to be wheatgrass and champagne, a combination that tasted even worse than it sounded. I forgave Windy-Mindy when the vitamins started coming on about twenty minutes later. Every cell in my body began sending my brain a jubilant message of thanks and goodwill, as well as suggesting, by the way, that they wouldn't mind getting to know every cell in Windy-Mindy's body if the opportunity should arise.

This wasn't my usual kind of trip and it made me suspect two things: (1) The tablets probably weren't Vitamin C and (2) if Windy-Mindy was on the same ride, it might explain her unlikely but undeniable interest in me.

Another possibility was that she had heard I was Jake Constable, a.k.a. the host of the party. From there she might have leapt to the not-unreasonable conclusion that the twenty-million-dollar mansion in which the festivities were taking place was also mine. Which was true, in a very temporary but excruciatingly legal sense.

The actual owner of the house, Mickey Wu, had hired me to look after it while he was out of town. For most of the evening, my flagrant abuse of this responsibility had precluded me from enjoying the party. Which was too bad since it was turning into a real killer.

The place was mobbed with people, a relief in those early evening "will-it-happen?" moments, but now a source of concern. I took it as a matter of faith that the front door was still on its hinges as I hadn't seen it close in hours. On the mezzanine, a velour-clad DJ was hunched over a laptop and two turntables, conjuring up humongous bass beats and mixing them with everything from sirens to symphonies.

The crowd was loving it, up and moving on every available horizontal surface, including the dining room table, much to the annoyance of the people clustered around it hoovering up lines of white powder.

When an albino wearing a lime-green Speedo and an impish grin threaded his way through the crowd on a Vespa, I found myself on the verge of questioning whether the party had been such a brilliant idea after all. He was travelling at a reasonable speed and using his horn judiciously but I still couldn't shake that harbinger-of-ill-fate feeling.

At least until I discovered Windy-Mindy and her narcotic vitamins. After that, I was blissfully surfing the moment, my worries gone and my eyes inexorably drawn to her endless curves as they took on a cotton candy glow. I frowned and shook my head, but the effect persisted.

I spent long, increasingly paranoid moments pondering whether an admixture of wheatgrass and champagne could give bourbon hallucinogenic properties until I noticed the sun winking at me from behind the skyscrapers of downtown Vancouver through the window behind her. I squeezed my eyes shut, hoping to banish this unwelcome party crasher. When I opened them, the sun was eclipsed by another—The Norwegian.

My first impulse was to go over and hug him, but I knew that was only Windy-Mindy's vitamins messing with my amygdala. My second impulse was to run.

It had been almost three years since I had seen my former business partner, and he hadn't changed a bit. The ornate black leather trench coat and vaguely Druidic hairstyle would have been comical on a smaller man less prone to violence. As he loomed over the crowd I tried to disappear within it. We hadn't parted on the best of terms.

I had brought him in on a deal that had started as a hobby for me, a way to use the inheritance I received from my grandfather—a couple acres of land on Hornby Island and a green thumb. Granddad grew prize-winning heirloom tomatoes there. People loved his tomatoes. I preferred marijuana. As did my friends, and their friends, and so on.

When I terminated our partnership, The Norwegian kept three hundred thousand dollars of my money and I kept my kneecaps, which seemed like a fair distribution of assets at the time. Deprived of "Granddad's Ganja", The Norwegian moved into harder drugs and I moved into a converted loft in a post-industrial neighbourhood in East Vancouver. I spent money, threw parties, started dating my real estate agent, wrote a screenplay, shredded a screenplay, married my real estate agent, spent the last of my money, got divorced by my real estate agent, became mildly depressed, and began perusing community college course catalogs. I was a phone call away from signing up for a denturist training program when my ex-wife/realtor lined me up with house-sitting gigs for her wealthy clients.

Clients like Mickey Wu, in whose house The Norwegian was now standing. He was nonplussed when he spotted me. Then his face lit up with the expression of affected innocence that always accompanied his most heinous acts.

My pocket vibrated. I dug out my phone to find a text from Richard.

there's a dead guy in the bathroom :(

I stared at the phone. Then I stared across the room at the bathroom door. The Norwegian was no longer standing in front of it. He had been replaced by Richard, who was staring back at me with an expression of genuine innocence and barely controlled panic.

Chapter Two

With the help of Richard and his partner, Dante, I managed to close down the party without anyone realizing there was a fresh corpse on the bidet. By the time we finished herding people out the door, the sun gained sufficient perspective to glare down at Mickey Wu's bathroom rather judgmentally.

Richard initially wanted to call the cops, but The Norwegian was long gone and I hadn't asked Mickey Wu if I could have friends over. I couldn't see the upside.

Richard accepted my decision stoically, feeling partially to blame for the mess in the bathroom since he was the one who talked me into having the party in the first place. I certainly saw it that way, but we had been friends since high school so I was willing to forgive a lot. Particularly when I needed help disposing of a corpse.

I had known Dante, his partner, only a few years but I trusted him because Richard did. The two of them had met at a Tae Bo class and quickly became partners in both the bedroom and business. Together, they were Buff—not only an accurate physical description of the two of them, but also the name of their high-priced house-cleaning business. It was conceived the night Richard made a losing bet on a pair of queens in a high stakes poker game. He and Dante cleaned the winner's condo in the buff, and paid for a trip to Palm

Springs with the tips they made. They went pro as soon as they got back.

The prospect of a post-party Buff Job had been instrumental in my caving to Richard's importuning to have a party in one of my clients' homes. I resisted for a long time, reminding myself that I now ran a legitimate business and partying in clients' homes was no longer encouraged. I had matured. But when Mickey Wu hired me to look after his place for a month, I found out I was wrong. I hadn't matured at all.

Mickey's mansion was hidden away behind a bamboo hedge of prehistoric dimensions. Its monolithic front doors opened up like a *Dwell* centerfold to reveal the Pacific Ocean. The stunning vista was minimally impaired by a sprawling leather sectional sofa, a three-story wall of glass, and a twenty-person hot tub—amenities that might sound grand, but looked trivial in contrast to the expanse of shimmering saltwater beyond. As I admired the polished cement floors, Richard's voice had whispered in my head, *indestructible…easy to clean…*

An hour later, that same voice had shrieked gleefully in my ear when I called to green-light the party. In exchange came Richard's assurance that he and Dante would clean up after themselves as well as everybody else. At the time I was envisioning little more than spilled drinks and sticky floors, but a promise is a promise.

After the last of the house pests had been chased away, Richard opened up the bathroom door and we stepped inside. Dante was the first to break the silence. "This is Italian marble," he said with an encouraging smile. "All that blood's going to wash right off."

"Anybody recognize him?" Richard asked.

No one spoke. Especially not Mickey Wu from where he lay on the bathroom floor, staring up at me with a glassy, accusatory expression.

As I leaned over the sink, I reminded the pale, sweaty guy

I saw in the bathroom mirror that Mickey Wu was out of town. It couldn't be him. It only looked like him. Don't get me wrong, it's not that I think all Asian men (or women) look alike. I'm not a racist or in need of glasses. Impaired, yes. Not to mention stressed out. Plus, the dead guy's facial features had been significantly reconfigured by a bidet-shaped dent in the side of his head. So when I saw a middle-aged Chinese man in a black suit and crimson tie lying on Mickey Wu's bathroom floor, I immediately thought of him. Generally, with nightmares it's not unreasonable to expect things to go from bad to worse.

"Do you think someone did that to him?" Dante piped up as he worried a fingernail with billboard-worthy dentition. He seemed a bit skittish, but Dante was always vibrating with kinetic energy. Given a German mother and an Italian father, the man was like a Dachshund crossed with a Ferrari.

"Possibly," Richard replied. "Or maybe he just OD'd and bounced off the porcelain on his way down." With the toe of his shoe, he coaxed a small bag of mossy green powder from beneath the corpse.

"The Norwegian was here tonight," I muttered as I splashed cold water on my face and dried it with one of the towels rolled and stacked in a small basket beside the sink. It was as thick and soft as a sheepskin. I was glad Mickey Wu wasn't dead. The linens bespoke a classy guy.

Richard looked aghast. "Why would you invite *him*?"

"You know I haven't talked to the guy in years," I told the mirror. "I have no idea how he heard about the party. But he was here, standing right outside this bathroom before you found our friend here."

Dante stamped his foot. "We should definitely call the police."

"It's up to Jake." Richard's tone had softened to something that sounded suspiciously like pity.

I understood where Dante was coming from but I couldn't go there. I didn't like the idea of ratting anyone out. Even The Norwegian. I downright hated the idea of him finding out about it. "No cops." I sighed, not entirely for theatrical effect. "If you guys want to get clear of this right now, I totally understand. Go ahead and take off."

For some reason they didn't, so I pushed my luck. "Anyone know how to dispose of a body?"

"What you need is a pig farm," Dante advised.

Richard rolled his eyes. "Do you see any livestock around here? Does Jake look like a farmer?"

Dante regarded me thoughtfully before shaking his head. "He's got more of a stevedore thing going on. Or maybe a park ranger on his day off."

Richard ignored him. "Sulfuric acid?"

Dante nodded thoughtfully. "Could work."

I looked at them blankly.

"Drain cleaner," Dante explained. "Dissolves hair in no time."

"I need to do more than denude the man."

Dante waved away my objection. "Hair, human body, same result. I saw it on *Breaking Bad*."

Personally, I didn't like how the show surreptitiously glorified drug dealers as libertarian anti-heros, but there was no denying that Bryan Cranston had been extremely believable as an expert chemist. "How much would we need?"

Dante eyeballed the body. "Forty or fifty gallons?"

"Gallons?" I asked.

Dante nodded.

I shook my head. "Any other ideas?"

"Burial, cremation, crushing, dumping, dissolution…" Richard recited.

I cast a wary glance in his direction. "Got some hobbies I don't know about?"

Richard held up his smartphone. "Wikipedia. Means of clandestine disposal of a human corpse. There's also space burial, dismemberment, disposal by exposure—anyone up for a trip to the Parsi Towers of Silence?"

Dante recoiled. "Is that the new club over on Robson Street? The one with the mimes?"

Richard reached over and gave Dante's shoulder a squeeze. "You know I would never ask you to go there, babe. The Parsi Towers of Silence are in India. The Zoroastrians leave their corpses there for vultures to..." He waggled his fingers. "... dispose of."

Dante perked up. "India does have great full moon parties."

I worked my temples, hoping to erase my incipient hangover, if not the last eight hours of my life. "This is getting us nowhere."

"Don't be so negative," Richard chided as he scrolled through Wikipedia. "What about burial at sea?"

I looked out the bathroom window and smiled back at the sunlight as it merrily danced across the ocean depths.

● ● ● ● ●

We immediately bogged down over logistics. Dante offered to go home to get his paddleboard but Richard said that was a rookie move. This prompted Dante to give Richard the silent treatment. Richard took the opportunity to expand on an idea of his own—head down to the Granville Island marina and rent a Cigarette boat so we could "Miami Vice the mo-fo."

Dante rejoined the discussion before I was forced to break it to Richard that the marina only rented thirty-horsepower fishing boats. "Take the guy to the hospital."

Richard gasped. "Is he still alive?"

I looked over, half-expecting to see a disfigured corpse shambling back to life before our eyes, but it remained motionless.

Dante rolled his eyes. "Hospitals handle ODs all the time, so they must have some kind of protocol for dealing with John Does."

Richard nodded thoughtfully. "They probably tag 'em and bag 'em without raising an eyebrow."

I raised one of mine. "Tag 'em and bag 'em?"

Richard grinned. "I re-watched *Platoon* last weekend."

"I don't know. It seems callous, don't you think? How would you like it if someone dumped you outside the door like a bag of garbage." I nudged the dead guy with my foot, but he didn't offer an opinion.

"How is it any worse than dropping him into English Bay?"

"They bury Navy officers at sea," Dante pointed out. "It's very classy."

Richard looked exasperated. "You just suggested dumping him at the hospital."

Dante shrugged. "Either way."

Refusing to concede defeat, Richard busied himself with his phone once more. "The marina only rents Boston Whalers," he reported in a disgusted tone. "And they cost sixty bucks an hour."

"Right then, St. Paul's it is."

"Grab his phone," advised Dante.

I felt disappointed in him. "I might be the kind of guy who'll dump a guy on the street, but I'm not the kind of guy who robs a guy before dumping him on the street."

He looked disappointed in me. "Don't *keep* the phone, dummy. Get rid of it. There might be something on it that shows he was planning to come here—texts, a calendar entry, that kind of thing."

"Ah," I glumly contemplated frisking the corpse. "Good point." Burial at sea was starting to sound pretty good again.

"Right, then. It's decided." Richard clapped his hands together. "And I'm famished, so can we please get this place cleaned up already? Breakfast at The Elbow Room on me when we're done."

Dante's face lit up. "I could absolutely devour a James Farentino right now."

"Does that one come with shrimp?" asked Richard.

"You're thinking of the Karen," said Dante.

Richard wrinkled his nose. "Gross."

Dante proceeded to go through the rest of The Elbow Room menu from memory as they exited the bathroom. I stayed. After taking a moment to steel myself, I wormed my hands down into the front pockets of the dead guy's disagreeably snug pants. His thighs were warm but his pockets were empty.

I was in the midst of wrestling him onto his stomach to check the back pockets when, from the living room, I heard Richard exclaim, "Mao Tse Thong!"

Startled, I let the body fall back to the floor and was rewarded with the muffled thunk of a hard object knocking against the tiles. A quick foray into his suit jacket pocket produced his phone and wallet. I hesitated only briefly before returning the latter and hurrying out the bathroom door.

Like I said, I was no thief.

Chapter Three

I came out of the bathroom and stopped short. This time there was no doubt about it—the guy staring at me accusingly was definitely Mickey Wu.

Standing beside him was a hefty slab of meat in a yellow Adidas tracksuit. He had eyes like marbles and waves of freshly permed, almost colourless hair cascading down to his triple-striped polyester. Cavernous nostrils quivered like they'd caught the scent of something to gnaw on. I was reminded of the time my Uncle Frank dressed his pitbull up as Gene Simmons for Halloween using a wig he found in a trunk at my granddad's cabin.

Richard was grinning happily at the two of them. Dante looked as confused as I felt. "So," he said, "did you enjoy the party?"

"Mr. Wu!" I yelped, but my warning came a moment too late. My heart commenced vigorous palpitations while my hand groped for the knob to pull the bathroom door shut behind me. "I didn't know you were home," I added to demonstrate that I remained in full command of the painfully obvious, if nothing else.

"I cut my trip short, as I e-mailed you last night. Who are these people? What has happened to my house?" Mickey Wu's face was rapidly taking on the colour of a debilitating aneurysm.

"I had a…small gathering," I replied, playing for time to see if his arteries held. "An indefensible violation of our agreement, I know, and I won't insult you by making excuses." Not that I could think of any anyway. "If you'd like to come back in a few hours, I assure you that we will have your house restored to exactly the way you left it." Corpse-free was what I was aiming for.

Mickey Wu stared at me. I wanted to believe that he might be considering my proposal but couldn't quite get there. I consoled myself by focusing on the positive: he hadn't called the cops. Yet.

I suspected that if the silence stretched on much longer, I might have an aneurysm of my own.

"I really like your underwear," Richard interjected.

Dante hissed at him, his eyes wide as full moons. I merely stared, listening with interest as my throat made a dry clicking sound.

"*What?* Don't you know who this is?" Richard beamed at Mickey Wu. "Mao Tse Thong, the Underwear King of Beijing!"

Much to my amazement, after a brief hesitation Mickey Wu bowed slightly. "That is not my actual name, but yes, I am he."

"What was your slogan again? Revolutionary comfort?"

"The Comfortable Revolution." Mickey Wu frowned. "How do you know this? My underwear is not available outside of China."

"I spent some time in Shanghai working as a model." Richard illuminated the room with one of his more modest smiles. "Did a few shoots for your 'Made in America' campaign."

"Mmm, that campaign was a substantial success." Mickey Wu inclined his head. "Thank you for your contribution."

"It was my pleasure. And may I say that you have a beautiful home here. I hope you'll allow us to restore it to its previous splendour." He cranked it up to matinee-idol smile. "It would be my privilege to work for you again."

Mickey Wu hesitated before turning back to me, his expression hardening. "Mr. Constable, this mess will be cleaned up immediately. You will then return your fee and I will never, I repeat never, see or hear from you again. Is that clear?"

"Absolutely." I couldn't believe my ears. I wanted to fly across the room and hug Richard.

"I'm going to my club for a steam. I will return in two hours," Mickey Wu announced, with a meaningful glance in my direction.

I was making preparations to relax when he started across the room toward me. When I didn't move, Mickey almost walked right into me before pulling up in annoyance. "Step aside," he snapped. "I must use the washroom before I depart."

I stood frozen with my hand clamped on the bathroom doorknob. "Wouldn't you rather use the ensuite in the master bedroom?"

"I would not." His eyes narrowed as he looked over my shoulder at the bathroom door. "Why?"

"Oh, it's just that this one is a bit of a mess and I'd like the chance to get it tidied up before you use it."

"Out of my way, Mr. Constable."

When I hesitated, Mickey Wu snapped his fingers. "Thaddeus!"

The tracksuit advanced on me like I was the last skirt at the barn dance. I had three inches on his six feet, but he had thirty pounds on my two hundred. When I bounced on my toes, the guy grinned like a hyena and high-stepped like a nervous foal. He was such a wonderful anomaly. Part of me wanted to sample his wares before he was summoned back to the Island of Dr. Moreau, but the rest of me was in enough trouble already. I let go of the doorknob and stepped out of our mutual employer's way. Thaddeus teased his perm while I rubbed at my sandpaper skull in frustration.

● ● ● ● ●

All things considered, Mickey Wu took it a lot better than I expected. He merely asked a very reasonable question: "Who is this man?"

"Honestly, I don't have a clue," I replied.

Mickey Wu studied me at length. "I believe you." He sounded like he actually meant it. "What happened to him?"

"Honestly, I don't have a—"

Mickey Wu's expression sharpened, cutting me off in mid-sentence.

I shrugged. "We found him this way. There was a bag of what looked to be drugs on the floor beside him. As you can see, he also took a nasty knock to the head. But don't worry, blood washes right off Italian marble," I added quickly.

"What exactly were you planning to do with him?" His voice was dangerously quiet.

"Take him to the hospital," I said. "We figured they would handle things from there."

Mickey Wu closed his eyes and kept them that way for awhile. "Unacceptable," he said at last.

"We also considered burial at sea," Dante murmured.

"Let me understand this," Mickey implored the ceiling. "While I was out of town you had some kind of unauthorized gathering in my house, during which a man was killed, either by a drug overdose or a blow to the head." His gaze descended upon me, equal parts wounded and withering. "Does this adequately summarize the service you have provided to me?"

I nodded.

"Get out of my house," he hissed. "All of you."

My mouth hung open for a few seconds waiting for the

words to start coming. "Sir, we would be more than happy to clean…"

"Your services are no longer wanted in any capacity Thaddeus, remove these men immediately."

Chapter Four

Richard swallowed a mouthful of the Lumberjack. "I thought that went pretty well."

With effort, I looked up from the untouched pancakes on my plate. "In what possible way do you think that went well?"

He looked around theatrically. "Are we sitting in a police station right now or are we enjoying a sumptuous breakfast at The Elbow Room?"

He had a point. "The Elbow Room," I conceded.

"And tonight, are you going to be chauffeuring a corpse around town or watching *Full Metal Jacket* at my place?"

Okay, two points. "*Full Metal Jacket.*"

Richard loved watching military movies. Mostly so he could point out scenes of what he described as "latent homosexuality." If I objected, he would assert unassailable expertise on the basis of what he referred to as his own blatant homosexuality. The thing was, I wasn't actually disagreeing with him. I just wanted him to shut up so I could enjoy the movie. However, as tiresome as it was, I would rather listen to Richard speculate on Stanley Kubrick's sexual hang-ups than hear the sound of a dead body rolling around the trunk of my car.

"I guess it turned out okay," I admitted.

Dante snickered. "I'd say amazingly well, seeing as how you complimented the man's underwear."

"*Because* I complimented the man's underwear," Richard corrected him. "Which did a lot more to win him over than Jake's pathetic *mea culpa* or you asking him whether he enjoyed the party."

Dante shot Richard a venomous look. "I'm really sorry about that, Jake. I thought I recognized Thaddeus from the party and assumed he had forgotten something and come back for it. I had no idea the man with him was Mickey Wu."

I waved my fork dismissively. "Don't worry about it. There was no way you could have known who he was. Lucky for us, Richard did."

"I couldn't believe it was actually him. It was like meeting a celebrity—he got a lot of media coverage while I was in Shanghai."

"For selling thongs?" I had a hard time imagining China's state-controlled media putting too many column inches into racy underwear.

"My Mandarin is pretty limited but I got the sense that most of the coverage was negative. I think he kind of stirred things up when he named them after Mao."

"But he still sold enough of them to buy a house like that?" asked Dante.

"Mao Tse Thongs were very much the thing for kids in their twenties trying to show everyone at the shopping mall how irreverent they were." Richard made a moue of distaste. "Personally, I found the things tacky and uncomfortable. Like someone took a BeDazzler to a jockstrap."

Chapter Five

After breakfast, my hangover tried to convince me to go home for a nap, but the four cups of Elbow Room coffee coursing through my system overruled it. Feeling jittery and paranoid, I decided now was the perfect time to go looking for Martin Farrell. They say the best hunters are able to think like their prey. Not that it would be particularly difficult to track him down, as he seldom left the three-block radius around his hotel room.

Martin was a rich kid from West Vancouver. I met him during his half-hearted pursuit of a Bachelor of Commerce at the University of British Columbia. He was one of my best customers, regularly buying in bulk for his entire dorm. As a graduation gift, I gave him a free ounce and his father gave him a partnership in his Mercedes dealership. Martin celebrated by taking a 500SL convertible off the lot and going out for an extended joyride before trading it for twenty pounds of weed. Unimpressed with his son's negotiation skills, Martin's father wasted no time in revoking the partnership. Undeterred, Martin continued on the same trajectory, which is to say a tailspin, eventually crash-landing on Vancouver's version of skid row—the Downtown Eastside. He now lived on an allowance secretly provided by his mom, more than enough to cover his insatiable appetite for intoxicants. I was confident he would still know how to contact The Norwegian.

I had left my car back in Point Grey, the leafy and luxurious seaside enclave where Mickey Wu resided, due to the lingering effects of bourbon mixed with Windy-Mindy's vitamins. Vancouver was recently named Canada's "most walkable city," but I suspected that was merely tourism board code for "least number of days snowboots are required." The west side of the city is comprised of hilly residential neighbourhoods like Point Grey, whose affluence increased in correlation with their proximity to the Pacific Ocean. Three bridges—Burrard, Granville, and Cambie—crossed False Creek to connect these neighbourhoods to downtown Vancouver, located on a peninsula in the Burrard Inlet. The peninsula is divided into two forests, one concrete, one wood. A multitude of handsome, modern towers—office, retail, residential—dominate the downtown skyline all the way down to the water, as if trying to glimpse their photogenic reflection, unaware that they are dwarfed and upstaged by the mountains and ocean that surrounded them. The second forest is a miraculously preserved thousand-acre swath of trees called Stanley Park, a prehistoric oasis of calm on the edge of the metropolis. Extending from its northern tip is the Lions Gate Bridge, which connects West and North Vancouver, gouged into the base of the North Shore Mountains on the far side of the Burrard Inlet. More bridges funnel traffic to the municipalities to the south and east—Richmond, Burnaby, Surrey, Delta—allowing almost three million people to move around the Lower Mainland. A surprising number of them do so in Teslas, BMWs, and Range Rovers, but the odd person is on foot.

After the party, a very sober Dante drove us downtown to The Elbow Room in Buff's purple Hummer. As far as I could tell, the man never drank anything stronger than protein shakes. He also required absolute silence when behind the wheel so he could focus—not on the road, but on the Gregorian chants he played while he drove. I should have taken a cab.

I was in the process of repeating this mistake. Fickle autumn sunshine had enticed me into an ambulatory search for Martin before abandoning me on grey, grimy Hastings Street amongst the clamorous dregs of the night shift. It was impossible to guess whether some of the revelers were in the final throes of their binges or just starting out, but they made me want to either swear off drinking entirely or have a stiff one immediately. Things quieted down as I moved east toward Main Street and the drunks ceded dominion to the junkies. Too easily, I fell into step with this herky jerky parade of worn and faded humanity running down their clocks.

Turning the corner, I almost tripped over the second cadaver of the weekend. This one was slumped against the wall of a pawn shop dressed in a grey twill pants and a navy blue blazer. I smiled with relief. "Hi, Martin, long time no see."

The cadaver didn't move a muscle, possibly due to their absence, but alert eyes the colour of tarnished silver spoons swivelled upwards. They registered no surprise. Martin was calibrated to expect the unexpected. "Hey, Jake," he muttered, barely moving his lips.

"How's life down there?"

"A bit tricky at the moment. I'm under surveillance."

I followed his gaze to a rusty Hyundai with no front bumper. A thicket of parking tickets festooned its cracked windshield. "Martin, that car is abandoned."

He smirked. "Sure it is."

Martin cherished his beliefs rather zealously. Best not to get sidetracked. "You seen The Norwegian lately?"

"I wish. He hasn't been around in weeks. Word on the street is he's still running on empty."

"You know how I can get in touch with him?"

"His number's in my phone."

"Great." I waited. The blue blazer lay dormant; the skin and bones within continued to obey Newton's first law of motion.

"Can you give it to me?" I pressed.

"Sorry, man. If I move, they'll be all over me."

Together, we watched a crow forage amongst the Hyundai's parking tickets until it found the one it was looking for and took wing.

"I really need his number."

"Left pants pocket."

Martin's thighs weren't as warm as the dead guy's had been, but his phone was there, as promised.

"So you want to get back into business with him now that he's hitting the big time, huh?"

"Not a chance." I stopped entering The Norwegian's number into my phone. "Didn't you just say he was out of product?"

"Has been. But he's put the word out that he's gonna be flush any day now. High grade dope, and plenty of it."

I slid Martin's phone into his jacket pocket. "You know heroin's not my scene."

"Not heroin. Opium, man. The Norwegian's gone exotic. Can't wait to get a taste."

"Sounds great, Martin. I wish you and The Norwegian all the best in your future endeavours." I started to turn away.

"Got any weed then? You still kind of owe me, you know."

Martin looked up at me with such a hopeful expression that a hairline crack spider-webbed its way across my left ventricle. I made a mental note to spackle it up with some cholesterol while watching *Full Metal Jacket* this evening. "Sorry, Martin. I'm running on empty myself these days. I don't even have the 500SL anymore."

He regarded me suspiciously. "What'd you do with it?"

"Took it up the coast. Got as far as Prince Rupert before trading it to a fisherman for a pickup truck full of fresh Dungeness crabs. Man, they were good. I definitely got the better end of that deal." I shook my head sadly. "It was a beautiful car but it just wasn't made for those roads. Take it easy, Martin."

The Mercedes was actually parked in my friend Bella's garage. I had enjoyed my joyride almost as much as Martin enjoyed his, but neither of us truly earned or appreciated the car. Bella's a mushroom-picker on Hornby Island and the 500SL gets her a twenty percent price bump from the fancy Vancouver restaurants that buy her fungi. When she was in town a few months ago making a delivery to a seafood restaurant, she took me for a ride. Aside from being richly redolent of morels, the 500SL is still in superb shape. Unlike Martin, she takes very good care of it and is way too smart to let me near the driver's seat.

Chapter Six

After flagging down a cab, I pulled out my phone, scrolled to "N" in my contacts and made the call I'd been dreading. It rang a couple times, just long enough for me to start hoping it might go to voice-mail.

"Hello?"

"Hey, Nina." I tried to sound upbeat. "How's the real estate game?"

"You asshole!"

I waited a few seconds, hoping she might calm down. Or hang up on me. The continued sound of agitated breathing suggested I was out of luck on both counts. "So I guess you heard from Mickey Wu."

"Damn right, I heard from him! What the hell did you do, Jake? I put my ass on the line when I recommended you to my clients."

This was true, of course, but it still rankled since it had been her idea in the first place. I knew she only did it so I wouldn't go after alimony, which I hadn't wanted any more than the house-sitting gigs. But I said yes anyway because I figured it would at least keep us in close contact. The closer the better.

I abandoned upbeat and took a run at maudlin. "I screwed up big time. I don't know what I was thinking. The thing is, I've been pretty down lately and Richard suggested we have a little get-together to cheer me up. It just got a tiny bit out of hand." Like most women, Nina loved Richard. As far as she was concerned, he could do no wrong.

"Don't feed me that baloney, Jake. Mickey Wu is threatening to call his lawyer!"

This got my attention. I swapped maudlin for earnest. "Listen, just give me a chance to tell you my side of things, Nina. And then maybe you can tell me what Mickey Wu said." She didn't immediately shut me down. "Why don't we grab a drink this afternoon?"

I noticed the cabbie monitoring my progress in the rear-view mirror. I could see he was pulling for me, so I gave him a wink to let him know I had the situation in hand.

Nina hung up on me.

The cabbie was still watching me. "Sounds good, see you there," I mumbled before lowering the phone.

As the cab dodged through traffic I stared at the phone, willing it to vibrate in my hand. To my surprise, it did. A text popped up on the screen.

Cactus Club, one hour

Nina has terrible taste in bars.

Nina has incredible taste in footwear. She was wearing a pair of biker boots that looked like they were made of brontosaurus hide stitched together with Janis Joplin song lyrics. Faded jeans and a tobacco-coloured cardigan sweater completed her disguise. No one would ever guess she was a one percenter. Not the outlaw biker kind, but something far more lucrative—one of Vancouver's top-grossing realtors. Her taste for casual attire wasn't a hindrance to her professional achievements since most of her clients lived in China. I'd like to say that hard work was the secret to her success, but I suspected it had more to do with having an uncle who was a card-carrying member of the Central Committee of the Communist Party.

Nina was polishing off a brace of sliders when I sat down at the table and fell in love all over again. She didn't look up until she had methodically finished chewing and swallowing the last bite of her burger. After carefully wiping her mouth with a napkin, Nina began slurping a Coke and glaring at me.

I ate the pickle from her plate while I considered how to proceed. I was prepared to confess my sins but I didn't know how much Mickey Wu had told her and saw no reason to overshoot the mark.

"So," she said after noisily dredging the ice cubes with her straw. "You're into snuff parties now?"

Everything, apparently, is how much Mickey Wu told her. I tried to look mortified as I studied the silverware and worked on a genuine-sounding, preferably exculpatory, explanation. When I had a rough draft in mind I looked up to discover that Nina was grinning.

This was unexpected. I'd anticipated a chewing out at least as bad as the sliders had received. Still, there was no harm in a show of contrition just to be on the safe side. "Listen, Nina, I'm truly sorry that I caused you grief. It was a hugely irresponsible, boneheaded move."

"Yup." Her smile persisted.

"But...you're not angry?"

She shook her head. "It's what you do, Jake. It would be naive of me to expect anything else. I am, after all, dealing with a semi-employed, semi-reformed drug dealer coming up fast on his forties."

"I am not!"

"Which part?"

I affected a wounded look. "I prefer to think of myself as a semi-retired bon vivant tenderly stirring the embers of his fiery youth."

Nina rolled her eyes. "Whatever gets you to sleep at night."

"*Deadwood* reruns and my vaporizer, mostly." I generally prefer to let sleeping dogs lie, maybe even curl up beside them for a power nap, but I needed to know where I stood with Nina. "I appreciate the vote of no-confidence in my character, but why aren't you more pissed off right now? Didn't you hang up on me an hour ago?"

Nina nodded. "And then I called my uncle to tell him what happened. Our family's reputation is serious business back in China, you know. It would be totally humiliating for him if word of your little stunt got back to my uncle's cronies. And my client list would dry up in no time."

"All of which suggests you should be seriously angry with me."

"Which I was. Right up until the moment I found out that Mickey Wu is a nobody. So my uncle's not worried about what he thinks or says."

"Seriously? I thought the guy was some kind of big shot back in China."

"Just because he's rich?" If it was possible to scoff sexily, Nina managed it. "Millionaires are a dime a dozen over there. Real power comes from knowing the right people."

"Like your uncle?"

Nina nodded. "And Mickey Wu doesn't. My uncle has never even heard of him."

Unbelievable. First Mickey Wu decides to clean up my mess for me, and now Nina isn't even mad at me for making it. Could I get any luckier today?

""So, Jake…" Nina whispered as she leaned toward me with a look on her face that sent my heart galloping. Maybe I could…

"Tell me about this dead guy."

"Oh, yeah. Him." My heart rate settled back down to a jarring canter. "Not much to tell. Richard found him on the bathroom floor. We think he might have OD'd."

Her expression morphed into one of distaste. Nina treated her body like a temple; we both did. Lamentably, she allowed no sacraments stronger than extra strength aspirin within it. "Was he a friend of yours? Or maybe a customer?" Her tone was cutting.

I didn't bother to look wounded. "You know I only ever sold weed, Nina. And I don't even do that anymore. I have no idea who the guy was."

"But don't you want to know?"

"Not especially." Digging for dirt didn't strike me as a particularly effective way of getting out of a hole.

Nina looked disappointed. Her attention wandered back to her phone, which had been having brief seizures on the table at regular intervals. She never left the thing alone for more than a few minutes. There had been times when I had resorted to texting her to get her attention while we were having dinner together. It was a sore spot between us but watching her fiddle with it now did remind me of something.

"I have his phone," I volunteered in yet another attempt to get her to focus on me.

Nina raised an eyebrow but didn't look up, leaving me uncertain as to which was the phone of interest, hers or the dead guy's. To find out, I put his on the table between us.

She put hers away and looked at me expectantly. I hesitated. All of a sudden I wasn't sure I wanted to know who the guy was. What if it turned out that I did know him and hadn't recognized him after his run-in with Mickey Wu's bidet? What if his wallpaper photo was a shot of his wife and infant daughter? What if it was bad karma to snoop in a dead guy's phone?

All good reasons to leave the thing alone. On the other hand, there was the way Nina was looking at me right now.

I picked up the phone and flipped it open. Then I glanced at Nina to confirm that she hadn't suddenly sprouted bangs, which I took as evidence that we hadn't instantaneously time travelled back to the nineties. And yet I was still holding a flip-phone. Too much had been happening in my bloodstream and Mickey Wu's living room for me to notice this when I grabbed it off the dead guy.

I gave myself over to a hot flush of nostalgia. I loved flip-phones. If you don't enjoy thumbing one of those babies open, you should see a doctor immediately because you're a little dead inside.

I closed and opened it a couple more times and grinned at Nina. She checked her watch.

On my side of the table, nostalgia gave way to consternation as I frowned at the device's tiny display lit up with ghostly blue glyphs. "Is this Mandarin?" I turned the phone so Nina could see it.

She squinted, then nodded, taking possession of both the phone and my frown. Silence reigned as she mashed the old-timey navigation buttons for a minute. "There's almost nothing on this thing. Just two measly photos."

"Of what?"

"This girl." Nina turned the phone around to show me a picture of a young Chinese woman wearing a Stanford School of Business sweatshirt. "Was she at your party?"

I studied the photo, disconcerted by the fact that there was something familiar about her. After a minute I shook my head. "No. Definitely not. I would've remembered her," I added, hoping to convince us both.

"Maybe she's his girlfriend," Nina suggested.

"I hope not, seeing as how he's dead. Besides, she's way too young for him. He must have been close to my age and she's what, maybe twenty, twenty-one?"

Nina rolled her eyes. "Middle-aged guy dates girl twenty years younger. Quick, call CNN." She returned her attention to the phone. "Hang on, this second picture is a bit more interesting."

Surprised by her enthusiasm, I studied it closely before announcing my conclusion. "It's a bank."

"Exactly. Maybe he was casing the joint." Nina's eyes sparkled. "And after robbing the bank he double-crossed his partner, but the partner caught up to him and killed him at your party."

I thought back to the dead guy's conservative black suit and barber school haircut. "This guy was more bank teller than robber. It's probably a picture of where he worked."

Nina yawned. "Boring. No texts, no contacts. Only two outgoing calls. Didn't this guy have any friends?" She glanced up. "Let's call the numbers and see who answers."

Before I could stop her, Nina pressed redial on the first number. Her expression grew puzzled.

"Who is it?" I didn't really want to know the answer.

"It's not calling the number."

"Must be broken. Too bad." I exhaled a gust of relief and disappointment and held out my hand, which Nina ignored. She wrestled with the phone until a small plastic piece popped off and fell to the floor.

"Or if it wasn't before, it is now." I contorted myself to reach under the table.

When I re-emerged with the piece, Nina was grinning triumphantly. "Mystery solved. No SIM card. You see what's going on here, right?"

"Ummm, not really."

"The phone has barely been used...the SIM card's gone.... It's obviously a burner." Nina's mouth tightened into a pout of disapproval I knew all too well.

"You think the dead guy was a drug dealer, don't you?"

"Correct." She looked stern, but also self-satisfied. Like a half-Chinese Nancy Drew, assuming the book jacket drawings from my mother's childhood collection were woefully inaccurate. I shook my head to clear out adolescent mental images of torpedo bras beneath pixie dust sweaters.

Nina mistook my gesture for an indictment of her deductive powers. "I suppose you've got a better theory?"

I remained silent while I tried and failed to come up with one. Unfortunately, the fact that The Norwegian had been loitering around the crime scene made Nina's all too plausible. His ability to handle turf wars had been the reason I had partnered up with him in the first place.

In a huff, Nina returned her attention to her phone and began scrolling through her calls list. This inevitably presaged an abrupt departure on her part. I endured this snub with increasing frequency toward the end of our marriage and it still drove me crazy. I decided to turn the tables on her and stood up. "Well, I've got to…"

"I knew it! Check this out." Nina appeared surprised when she noticed I was standing. "Or did you have to rush off somewhere?"

I mumbled an incoherent equivocation and sat down again. "What have you got?" I nodded toward her phone.

"These outgoing calls on the dead guy's phone, one of the numbers looked familiar." She handed the phone back to me.

Both calls had been made on the night of my ill-fated party, one right after the other. The first call lasted six minutes. The second was less than a minute and the number was familiar to me as well—it was The Norwegian's. I groaned. "I recognize it, but how do you…?"

"So I checked my call records and, sure enough, here it is." Nina held up her phone to show an incoming call from the first number, logged only a few hours earlier.

I swallowed my question about The Norwegian and asked a different one instead, even though I didn't want to know the answer. "Whose number is it?"

"Mickey Wu's!"

This time Nina's breathy excitement did nothing for me. My heart was beating fast again, but it felt more like an incipient anxiety attack. A roller derby of confused thoughts and questions began careening around my head. At least the call to The Norwegian explained how he had found out about the party. Was it possible that one of his customers was also a friend of Mickey Wu's? Maybe the dead guy had called Mickey (prior to becoming dead, of course) to ask why he wasn't at his own party. Which would also explain Mickey Wu's early return. But if that was the case, why had Mickey acted surprised about the party? More importantly, why hadn't he recognized the dead guy?

I noticed that Nina was standing up. "You're leaving?" I was immediately annoyed with myself for asking the same old question in the same old tone of voice. "We still haven't figured out who the dead guy is."

"Just call Mickey Wu and ask him," she replied in a tone that was also familiar. It was the one she used when talking to her more obtuse clients on the phone. "Gotta run. Seeya, Jake."

I was still cataloguing all the reasons that call seemed like a bad idea when the waiter brought over Nina's bill.

Chapter Seven

It was late afternoon by the time I finally arrived home. After a power nap and a shower, I headed for Richard's place, stopping off to pick up curries and Kingfisher beers.

Richard gave me a disapproving look as he let me in. "That stuff is going to kill you one day."

"The beer?"

"The food."

"Aside from the goat, it's mostly vegetables and chickpeas. I thought you told me I should eat more of this stuff."

"In salads. Not swimming in ghee."

"So you don't want any?"

Richard put his hands on his hips and pursed his lips. "Where's it from?"

"Vij's. Where else?"

He snatched the take-away containers away from me and headed for the kitchen.

"Aren't you worried about killing yourself?" I called after him, tossing my jacket on the floor as soon as he was out of sight. Richard kept his condo in a state more akin to performance art than comfy digs. Where my place had an exposed brick wall authentically salvaged from the backside of a blast furnace, Richard and Dante spent an entire weekend creating an "accent wall" from bamboo they had personally macheted out of a jungle in Thailand. The furniture was sleek and modern—mostly teak, some walnut, swaddled where necessary in a colour palette of pale greens and greys. The walls were art gallery white, the paintings vivid and oversized. The floors were reclaimed hardwood, invariably clear of any visual impediments to the appreciation of their grain. Except when I was visiting.

"I exercise, take vitamins. It's you I'm worried about. When was the last time you went for a jog?" he called back over the clanking of dishes being removed from cupboards.

"I think it was grade seven. But I went for a nice, long walk today. Met an old friend, got The Norwegian's phone number."

The rattle of cutlery abruptly ceased. Richard's head reappeared. "Why on earth would you do that? Tell me you're not planning to confront him about what happened at the party."

"Hell, no. But if Mickey Wu decides to send the cops after me, I may have to point them in his direction."

His eyebrows formed disapproving auburn arches, though I wasn't sure whether it was because of what I said or the fact that he instantly spotted my coat on the hallway floor. "You're seriously considering ratting The Norwegian out to the cops? Maybe it won't be your diet that kills you after all."

"I'm not ratting him out," I replied heatedly, joining him into the kitchen. "But if the cops suddenly turn up at my door wanting to talk about a murder rap, I'm damn sure going to mention that he was there."

Richard said nothing and busied himself with the food.

"You have a better idea?"

"Anything that doesn't involve fingering The Norwegian sounds like a more palatable option to me." He sighed. "Didn't I warn you about getting involved with that man?"

"You did. And you were right. As I've admitted many times in the past. But it's not like I'm talking about going back into business with him."

"Good. Because I recall that the only thing that stopped him from breaking your legs at the end of that little misadventure was a three-hundred-thousand-dollar severance package, when you were the one who quit. What are you going to do if he finds out you ID'd him to the police?"

"It's not going to happen." I was not an optimist by nature, but I was even less a planner. The only thing I knew for sure was that I would do everything in my power to avoid talking to the cops about The Norwegian under any circumstances. But if I couldn't avoid it, and worse yet, The Norwegian found out about it, I'd burn that bridge when I came to it.

"This is your plan?" Richard muttered, speaking his mind as usual, and seemingly reading mine.

Not enjoying the incredulity he was serving up with the saag-paneer, I switched from defence to offence. "You'd at least back me up, wouldn't you?"

He paused, looking thoughtful. "Well...I didn't actually *see* The Norwegian at the party."

I scowled at him.

Richard reached over and rubbed my stubble-covered head playfully. "Oh, don't be so dramatic. Of course I'd back you up with the police. But if Mickey Wu was going to call them, don't you think he would have done it right away?"

I shrugged. "He's threatening to call his lawyer. If that happens, I doubt the cops will be far behind."

Richard's expression became serious. "He told you that?"

"No, I heard it from Nina."

Richard's expression became pained. "You talked to Nina?"

"I wanted to 'fess up and do damage control before she heard about it from Mickey Wu. No such luck."

He opened a beer and handed it to me. "You poor thing. Have a slug of this and tell the Big Dick all about it. How'd it go?"

I grinned. "Surprisingly well."

After I provided an executive summary of my lunch date with Nina, Richard added a summary of his own: "You've got more than your fair share of luck, my friend."

"Turns out some of it's even good."

Richard nodded. "Assuming this sordid little episode heralds the end of relations with your ex."

I finished my beer and changed the subject. "So are we going to watch this movie or what? When will Dante get here?" The pair were close to inseparable but they drew the line at cohabitation. It was one of Richard's "Ten Commandments For Maintaining A Healthy Relationship," ranking just below "Have Sex With Whomever You Want, But Not Breakfast Afterwards" and just above "To Each Their Own Tube Of Toothpaste."

"He's not coming. The only Kubrick film he'll watch is *Dr. Strangelove.*"

Richard took one look at my pained expression and raised his hand. "I know, I know. Don't say it." His tone bespoke the long-suffering nature of love. I didn't know whether to envy or pity him.

After liberating a bottle of single malt from Richard's liquor cabinet, we settled in for what proved to be a thoroughly therapeutic cinematic experience. *Full Metal Jacket* put our weekend's comparatively negligible body count into perspective.

Chapter Eight

After an evening at Richard's immaculate condo, I was shocked by how messy my place was. Particularly since I hadn't left it that way. I couldn't even blame my roommates since I didn't have any. At least now I knew how Mickey must have felt when he returned to find his house trashed by uninvited guests.

Entering the living room, I was relieved that my two prized possessions had escaped unscathed—a 1968 Eames Lounge Chair (rosewood frame with the original down-filled cushions) and my aquarium of neon tetras. I dropped my butt into one and stared at the other. After a moment, I noticed a black object roughly the size of a TV remote control lying amongst the plants at the bottom of the aquarium.

The fish darted away from the net in little iridescent flashes of blue and red as I scooped what was in fact my TV remote control out of the water. After drying it off on my shirt, I tried a few buttons. Nothing happened. I suspected the remote was toast, but couldn't be certain since the TV was gone.

I tended to watch the fish more than the television anyway. I also took solace in knowing the thief would have to get up off the couch every time he wanted to change the channels.

I was just about to sit down again when I heard a faint crunching sound in the kitchen. Fishing around in the aquarium had already blown any stealth advantage I might've had, so

I opted for speed instead. I dropped the remote and ran back to the front hall to retrieve the Louisville Slugger I kept in the closet in case I ever took up baseball, or started dealing again.

I choked up on the bat and headed for the kitchen.

It was ugly. Dishes were strewn across the countertop and the cabinets were almost empty. Nothing unusual about that, but my extensive collection of almost-empty cereal boxes had been thrown to the floor, spilling their meagre contents across the tile. Sitting in the middle of it all was Mr. Saturday Night, my upstairs neighbour's Siamese cat. He stopped eating Honey Nut Cheerios long enough to stare at me cross-eyed.

I loosened my grip on the bat. "You want some milk with those?"

In accordance with the feline prime directive, Mr. Saturday Night ignored me. The fact that he was making himself at home made me suspect that the burglar no longer was, but I searched the loft anyway.

It was empty. There were no signs of forcible entry on the front door or bedroom windows, but many of extreme prejudice toward my belongings. In every room, the contents of drawers and cupboards had been dumped out.

I returned to the kitchen to see if Mr. Saturday Night was ready to talk. This time when he saw me, he hissed, jumped up on the kitchen table and disappeared out the open window onto the fire escape. Maybe he wanted milk after all. Mr. Saturday Night's rude exit at least answered the question of how the burglar had gotten in.

Looking around the room, I noticed that a lone box of Lucky Charms remained standing at the back of the cupboard. Awash in hope and dread, I went over and pushed it aside. My heart leapt when I saw that the mason jar that lived behind it was still there, its contents unmolested. I smiled back at the leprechaun on the box. "Impressive," I told him. "Not only are your wares magically delicious, but they actually work too."

To celebrate, I took the box and the jar down from the cupboard and started looking through the mess for a cereal bowl and some rolling papers.

For the second time in twenty-four hours I made the questionable decision not to call the cops. Partly because I couldn't decide where to hide my mason jar, but also because little of value appeared to be missing. Sure, my television was gone, but it was a five-year-old Sanyo with a replacement cost that was undoubtedly less than my insurance deductible. I could only assume the intruder had left my Rega turntable, along with the Anthem amp and B&W speakers, out of respect.

The half-assed nature of the plundering combined with the full-assed nature of the mess made me question whether I was dealing with a straightforward burglary. One unpleasant alternative that came to mind was that The Norwegian stopped by to deliver a message. Although the continued presence of my stash led me to discount this possibility.

After a cursory attempt at tidying up, I grabbed the mason jar and retired to my bedroom, screwing over future Jake yet again by leaving the mess for him to deal with.

Chapter Nine

Sleeping half the day felt like a reasonable way to balance the ledger after two exhausting nights of skullduggery. It also felt damn good. Until I opened my eyes and took a fresh look at my place. After cursing past Jake for his laziness, I spent the afternoon cleaning the loft. The results weren't up to Buff standards, but at least the floors were once again navigable.

I was running out of reasons not to go get groceries when Richard called to report a higher-priority domestic issue. "Jake, you're not going to believe this but…"

"Let me guess—your place got broken into?"

There was a brief silence on the line. "How the hell did you know that?"

"I'll explain when I get there."

I took Richard's word for the fact that his condo had been similarly trashed, because he and Dante already had it back to looking like a display suite by the time I arrived. So much for comparing crime scenes.

"It's not healthy for you guys to bring your work home like this, but it would be great if you could take it over to my place."

Dante brushed off my suggestion with his ostrich feather duster, but Richard latched on. "So your place got burgled as well?"

"Burgled is a generous description. Violated might be more apt. Whoever did it made a real mess—emptied all the closets and cupboards, but as far as I can tell nothing much is missing."

Richard adjusted a piece of art on the wall. "Same here, now that you mention it. That's why I haven't called the police. What little I could claim on insurance would be clawed back in premiums anyway. Who needs the hassle?"

Looking around, I noted with relief that Richard's giant television was still securely bolted to his wall. At least our movie nights weren't going to be cancelled. His Bang & Olufsen stereo also remained, along with the art and wine, which Richard assured me was also of significant value.

"Do you think the break-ins are connected?" asked Dante.

I spread my hands. "Could be. The M.O. is pretty similar, and it's not like we're neighbours."

"Maybe it has something to do with what happened to that guy at the party," Richard said uneasily.

Dante stopped sweeping. "What if The Norwegian did this?"

"I wondered about that but it doesn't feel right. The Norwegian's preferred medium is people, not property. He's all about face-to-face intimidation." I nodded in agreement with my own analysis. "The Norwegian is much more likely to break your legs than your dishes."

For some reason, my friends weren't reassured by my theory, so I tried again. "If this is connected to our party, why would they only break into Richard's and my places? Why not Dante's as well?"

Dante's eyes went wide. "I haven't been home yet. We came here straight from our last job."

• • ● ● •

Dante was so delighted by the pristine, unviolated state of his abode that he offered to make us dinner to celebrate as well as to console us on our own misfortunes.

Over a truly excellent seafood stir fry, we discussed what to do about the break-ins. Nothing, is what we decided. If there was no need to call our insurance companies, there was no need to call the cops. The last thing we wanted was to bring them into the picture if all this was connected to our ill-fated party. Our places had been trashed, not looted. If this was done to send a message, we didn't know what it was. If the intruder was looking for something, maybe he or she found it, since Dante's place hadn't been hit as well. It was time for everyone—except the dead guy—to move on with their lives.

Chapter Ten

This time when I got home I felt more depressed than surprised by how messy my place was. The door being kicked in was the tip-off. There are a variety of ways a three-hundred-pound man can get what he wants, but stealth isn't one of them.

The Norwegian greeted me with a wave. "You should get some new furniture, Constable. This chair must be twenty years old." The rosewood creaked ominously as he spun around.

"Closer to fifty, so go easy on it, would you?"

He looked hurt. "Do you think I'm getting fat? I recently acquired an exercise bike from a former customer. Should I give it a try?"

"Is this customer 'former,' as in no longer a patron, or no longer of this world?"

"Since when do you want to know the details of how I handle collections?"

It was a fair point. The Norwegian used to handle sales and distribution for "Granddad's Ganja." A purebred Viking with an MBA from the University of Oslo, he was the best and only applicant for the job when my business got big enough to attract the attention of the Serious Criminals. It was undeniably a rash application of "if you can't beat them, join them" logic on my part. Life is often less about making good decisions than figuring out how to live with bad ones.

After The Norwegian came on board, we both rolled up our sleeves and got our hands dirty—me on Hornby Island tending the crops, and him dealing with the turf war my success had incited. Things quickly came to a head when an Indo-Canadian gang leader named Mangalmor mocked The Norwegian's leather cowboy hat—I never saw either one of them again. After that, the only criminal element left to bother me was The Norwegian himself. His incessant lectures on "exploiting market synergies" and "realizing economies of scale" were tedious, and the assigned readings incomprehensible since the textbooks were in Norwegian. When he presented me with a business plan to make the entire operation more efficient, it was time for us to part ways. The party was over.

"New topic then. Why are you here?"

"I just wanted to find out what you're doing with yourself these days." The Norwegian picked up the mason jar from the floor beside the chair and raised an inquiring eyebrow.

"Strictly for personal use," I assured him.

"And you're not thinking about branching out?"

"Into what?"

The Norwegian's eyes narrowed. "Anything that might encroach on my business interests."

Opium? Murder? I wanted to assure The Norwegian that he had those markets cornered almost as much as I craved a speedy conclusion to his visit. I shook my head.

The Norwegian gave me a knowing look. One of his standard intimidation tactics, but still unsettling because it meant he was contemplating an act of violence to test the veracity of something he'd just been told. I stared out the window, hoping he was feeling lazy.

"Okay," he said at last. "I believe you. I just had to be sure after running into you last night."

I exhaled the tension I hadn't even realized I was holding. "Hey, I was as surprised as you were. How'd you hear about my party anyway?" I already knew the dead guy had called him, but I was hoping The Norwegian might tell me who the man was, or how he ended up dead.

"That was your party?" The Norwegian's expression brought to mind a stormy night at Stonehenge, charcoal sketches of Neandertals, the Dark Ages. "I thought I saw your fancy-boy friends there. Dick and Donny, yes?"

"Richard and Dante, yes. So you didn't know I was the one, uh...hosting it?"

"I didn't even know there was going to be a party. I was there to do a favor for my boss." He heaved himself up and headed for the door, pausing at the threshold to give me a look heavy with disappointment. "This is the second time you've messed up my business, Constable. You know I can't let that kind of thing go unpunished. People will say I've gone soft."

I said nothing. As far as I was concerned, I had already paid plenty for terminating our partnership. The Norwegian had obviously found a new supplier, but beyond that, I didn't know what business The Norwegian was referring to, or how I had screwed it up. At least this time he didn't leave with three hundred grand of my money. He did, however, take what little peace of mind I had left. And that was priceless.

Chapter Eleven

The next morning I was filled with regret as I contemplated my recent mistakes. What could have possessed me to eat the last of my Lucky Charms before going to bed? As I showered, I debated between the old greasy diner on the next street that does great eggs but terrible coffee and the nouveaux greasy diner on the next block that has excellent coffee but was guilty of transgressions such as serving me salmon with my eggs. I like salmon and I like eggs, but not together. Never together.

It occurred to me that I wouldn't be able to make it an entire block without coffee anyway. As is so often the case, the answer became obvious once I got my priorities figured out. I got dressed and headed toward the kitchen feeling positive. Sure, the weekend had presented me with a few problems, but maybe the week ahead would offer up some solutions.

My optimism lasted as far as the living room, where I found two well-dressed Chinese men waiting for me. I was pleased to see that both were still breathing and neither was Mickey Wu.

"Neon tetras," said the one standing by the aquarium. "Beautiful fish." His face was teflon smooth, putting him somewhere between twenty-five and fifty years old, and the way he smiled made me suspect it was his go-to expression. Not exactly fake, but definitely pro forma. As if anything more emotive would only complicate things. His outfit was cut from the same cloth. Conservative black suit, white shirt, mid-fat tie in movie-usher red. The non-look completed by black socks and off-brand oxfords. Camouflage for a wedding, a funeral, or anything in between.

"And this chair," the other cooed. "It is perfection." No smile to sweeten things here. Just a statement of fact. He wore a similar uniform, but this one came with a chip on the shoulder. His cheeks were sunken, the muscles atrophied long ago, but his jaw was strong and well used. I could almost hear the echoes of his teeth grinding from the night before. Unless it was the relentless sound of him chewing things over. Either way, when this man spit, the shrapnel caused collateral damage. His world was clearly a serious place, both the good and the bad. Fortunately, the Eames chair was seriously good. I noted with appreciation that he had removed his shoes before putting his feet up on the ottoman.

"You guys want some coffee?" I asked as pleasantly as I was able before having had any myself.

It was lucky they didn't because my espresso maker only delivers three shots at a go. I headed into the kitchen and fired it up. When it began hissing at me from the stovetop I emptied the contents into my Columbo mug, which I noticed had a new crack in it from the previous day's domestic disturbances. I carried it back to the living room feeling put out.

"Please excuse our unannounced entrance," said the fish lover. "Your door was ajar." He looked around with concern. "Have you been robbed?"

"Good question. Listen, I'm all out of Lucky Charms, so if you guys don't want coffee I'm not sure what I can offer you." I slurped mine noisily.

"Information is all we require," said the Eames fan. "What can you tell us about your employer, Mickey Wu?"

Grudgingly, I dropped onto the couch. "Well, first of all, he's no longer my employer."

"You have been fired?" The fish lover's tone suggested concern, but his smile showed barely a ripple at the prospect of my ill fortune.

"Let's just say he made it clear that he no longer requires my services."

"And you are a drug dealer, is that correct?"

The one in my Eames chair had asked the question so casually that I couldn't quite believe my ears. "Run that one by me again?"

This time he frowned, but more out of confusion than hostility or accusation.

"He is asking whether you sell drugs," the fish lover said mildly. "More specifically, we wish to know whether you have sold any illegal drugs to Mr. Wu."

I looked them both over again. The suits were cheap and the haircuts matched. The oxfords were scuffed and sensible. "Are you guys cops?"

The fish lover smiled. "We are not police officers, I assure you. Nor are we interested in holding you accountable for your criminal activities. We are here investigating a broader issue pertaining to Mr. Wu."

Somehow I didn't find his assurance all that reassuring. "If you're not cops, then who the hell are you?"

There was a brief, rapid exchange in Mandarin before the fish lover responded. "We are government representatives from the People's Republic of China tasked with investigating Mr. Wu's citizenship and immigration status."

"Can I see some ID?"

The fish lover smiled. "Of course."

I took my time inspecting their identity cards, but not long enough to learn to read Mandarin. They looked real enough, but that didn't mean much. I knew a guy who knocked off totally convincing IDs for fifty bucks a pop.

"Okay, so you're the People's representatives. But why are you asking me questions?"

"We are hoping that you might be of some assistance in establishing some context relating to Mr. Wu's current situation here in Canada."

"Having something to do with me being a drug dealer? Which I'm not, by the way. Not that it's any of your business."

The Eames fan looked so bummed out that I almost offered to roll him a joint. "We ask because if Mr. Wu is involved in any illegal activities here, his status here would be in jeopardy," he explained. "In addition, it is of significant general concern to China any time one of its prominent expatriates is connected with criminal activities or persons."

"Sorry, can't help you. I'm a house-sitter, not a dealer. Which means my job is to go into my clients' houses when they're not there. So I've had very minimal contact with Mr. Wu since we first met a few weeks ago."

"Do you happen to know whether he is a Canadian citizen?" the Eames fan asked.

I shook my head. "No clue."

There was that frown again. His confusion dissipated after the fish lover said something to him in Mandarin, at which point he gave a curt nod.

"As a house-sitter, you bring in the mail for your clients, is that correct?" he asked.

"Sure, that's part of the job." My stomach grumbled in a way that adequately expressed my growing impatience.

"Did you happen to notice any communications from your government's immigration department? Or anything from family members? Personal correspondence from persons with the surname 'Wu'? Business contacts, perhaps?"

"Come on, guys, I can't discuss that kind of thing with you." I showed them a disappointed look of my own. "What kind of house-sitter would I be if I violated my clients' privacy like that?"

They had the decency, or maybe just the acting chops, to look chagrined. "We understand entirely," said the fish lover.

"You've been very kind to speak with us at all. May I ask just one more thing?"

"If you make it quick." I glanced at my hairy wrist. "I'm running late for breakfast with George."

With the elegant economy of a man who worked with his hands for a living, the Eames fan produced a grainy blow-up of the kind of mug shot featured on driver's licenses and security passes the world over. "Have you ever seen this man before?" he asked, his expression neutral and his tone polite.

I frowned thoughtfully at the picture, making a show of studying it for a moment before I shook my head. "Who is he?" I asked, hoping to find out something beyond what I already knew—he had left his mortal coil on Mickey Wu's bathroom floor.

"Just someone who might have had some contact with Mr. Wu." The fish lover treated me to a parting smile, but cheek fatigue was starting to show. "Goodbye, Mr. Constable. Thank you very much for your time."

Chapter Twelve

After giving my visitors a few minutes to vacate the premises, I headed out the back door of my building and down the alley toward the diner.

On my way past the dumpster I noticed some idiot had dumped a bunch of rotting vegetables into it, even though there was a compost bin right next to it. Even more annoyingly, all that fetid spinach had made a real mess of my television. I hoped my burglar hadn't quit his day job. And if he had, I wondered if it was available since I was probably going to have to start looking for a new one myself. And after that, a new TV.

The diner was a cozy little spot with six booths done up in battle-scarred formica and blistered red vinyl. Five were empty. I took a seat at the counter and ordered breakfast from George, the octogenarian server. Eggs poached soft, wheat toast, grilled tomato, bacon. Coffee and ice water. Same as always.

George wrote it all down. When he was finished, he frowned at his pad for a moment. After making a few corrections, he nodded with satisfaction, tore off the sheet and stuck it on the order rack behind him. Same as always.

I waited until the second round of coffee entered my bloodstream before contemplating the possible implications of the morning's unexpected interrogation. The call to Mickey Wu from the dead guy's phone fit with my visitors' suspicion that the two men had been in contact. If it turned out that the dead guy was a friend of Mickey Wu's rather than a guest of mine, I had a sinking feeling that it would mean more trouble for me. But why hadn't Mickey recognized him? Had the bidet reconfigured the guy's face that significantly? It had been a bit hard to tell with all the blood.

Of more personal concern was the question of how the People's Republic of China came by the notion that I was a drug dealer. I only knew one person who had any connection to the Chinese government, but I couldn't bring myself to believe that Nina would drop the dime on me. She had already assured me that what had happened at Mickey Wu's was a non-issue as far as her uncle was concerned, and back when we were together, Nina had been as keen as I was to keep my occupation a secret.

Much to my annoyance, my phone started going off just as George arrived with my breakfast. Together, we listened to the muffled rendition of the Bee Gees' "Stayin' Alive" coming from my pants until the call went to voice-mail.

"You bet your ass," George whispered hoarsely as he shuffled off to get the coffeepot.

While I was mopping up the last of the yolk with the last of the toast, my phone serenaded me a second time. Both callers left voice-mails.

The first message was from Mickey Wu. I doubted it was good news but I couldn't know for sure since he employed one of the annoying tactics of successful people and refused to invest the few courteous seconds required to leave an informative message. "Please call me immediately, Mr. Constable."

The second voice-mail was from Nina. She had Mickey Wu beat on brevity, if not politeness: "Call me."

When I disconnected from voice-mail, I saw that Richard had texted me while I was listening to the messages:

Dante is missing! call me asap

I dialed Richard's number first. I hated calling people back when they didn't say what they wanted to talk about.

Chapter Thirteen

"Dante is missing!" Richard yodelled into my ear.

"Yeah, I got your text. That's why I called. So what happened? He went out for more Windex this morning and didn't come back? Did you guys have a tiff or something?"

"No, we didn't have a tiff," Richard replied acidly. "He didn't show up for work today and he's not answering his phone."

"I thought you spent the night at his place?"

"No, I went back to my place last night to finish cleaning up. Maybe around 11 p.m." Richard's tone expressed disappointment in my telepathic abilities.

"Okay, so what time did he drop off the radar?"

"Well…I tried to call him around 10 a.m., after he didn't show up for our job at Sunshine Holly's penthouse."

This new information got my attention. "The actress? I didn't know you guys did her place. Nice score."

"She prefers the term 'visual performance artist', but 'cokehead skank' would also fit the bill. You should see some of the messes we have to deal with. Especially after Samhain."

"Sam who?" I was struggling to keep up as I waved my empty coffee cup at George.

"Samhain. It's a pagan celebration of the dead. Sunshine decided she was a Wiccan after she played the Wicked Witch of the Web on that Internet serial last year."

"Missed that one. But have you considered the possibility that Dante actually arrived early and she has something to do with his disappearance?"

"This isn't a joke, Jake." Richard's voice was taut enough to adequately reinforce the message.

"Okay, okay. Calm down. Maybe he just stayed home sick or something."

"He's not at home."

"How do you know?"

"Because I'm at his place right now." Richard let out a shuddering breath. "And it's been broken into."

I stopped fantasizing about Sunshine Holly and gave Richard my full attention. "You might've wanted to open with that."

"It's worse than ours, Jake. His door has been forced open and I think there might have been a fight or something. It's hard to be sure because the place is a total mess." Richard paused to steady his voice. "I'm worried, Jake. I want to call the police."

They say not knowing what happened is the worst part about having someone you love disappear, so I decided to take a gamble. "You guys might have been right about The Norwegian being behind all this. He kicked my door in and was waiting for me when I got home last night."

"Oh, God, are you okay? We need to call the cops immediately."

I never had been much of a gambler. "Hold on, I'm not telling this to alarm you. The Norwegian didn't hurt me or anything. He just wanted to know what I was doing these days."

"The guy breaks into your place just to find out how you're doing, and you don't think that's going to alarm me?"

"Not how I'm doing, *what* I'm doing. When he saw me at our party it made him suspicious that I might be getting back into the weed business. He spotted you guys there, too, so I'm saying…I don't know…maybe he also broke into Dante's place."

"But Dante was never *in* the business," Richard protested.

"True, but The Norwegian is the kind of guy who likes to intimidate first and think things through later. Maybe he was following me around and saw us go to Dante's place last night."

"None of this is making me feel any better, Jake." Richard's words came out so rapidly that it took me a few seconds to parse them.

"I don't think bringing in the cops is going to accomplish that either. If we tell them about The Norwegian, we also have to tell them about the party at Mickey's. Once we're into that, it's going get really tricky not to mention the cadaver in the bathroom. And I'm pretty sure that a dead body trumps a missing one in copworld."

Richard didn't say anything right away, so I did. "You said you weren't even sure there had been a struggle, right? So how about this—let's give Dante a bit more time to resurface on his own. In the meantime, I'll reach out to The Norwegian to see if I can figure out for sure whether he's involved. If neither of those pan out, we'll notify the cops."

"If Dante is still missing by the time I'm done working, I'm making the call." Richard sighed. "I need to go back to Sunshine's penthouse to finish sanitizing her gymnasium anyway. After that, I'm coming straight back here."

"Okay, I'll meet you at Dante's right after work."

I wasn't as worried about Dante's safety as Richard was. They were not only one of those rare and admirable couples who don't crowd each other, but also those rare and admirable humans who don't take their work too seriously. My hope was that Dante was simply AWOL and would turn up on his own.

Which didn't explain the break-in, but it was going to have to get to the back of the line of unanswered questions and wait its turn. I had done a better job of convincing Richard than myself that The Norwegian had broken into Dante's, but it was the most optimistic possibility I could think of. Even if he had gotten it into his head to kick down Dante's door, I was reasonably confident that he wouldn't go so far as to hurt him. When it came to making people disappear, The Norwegian was all business. And Dante had nothing to do with his.

A promise is a promise, though. I had told Richard that I would see what I could find out. I called The Norwegian's number. It went straight to voice-mail without giving me any time to get ready to leave a message, so I was forced to take a page out of Mickey Wu's uninformative book. "It's Jake. Call me back."

Next, I called Nina back. Also straight to voice-mail. This time, I hung up without leaving a message. It was the only way I could beat her in the brevity department.

Which left Mickey Wu.

I pocketed my phone. I had time to kill and a growing list of questions about a growing list of crimes. Maybe I could answer a few of them by returning to the scene of the first one. Or maybe not. Either way, I still needed to pick up my car.

Chapter Fourteen

When I ventured outside to find a cab, I discovered a glorious autumn day—a rare and precious thing in Vancouver, where most years the season was cancelled on account of rain. The breeze was warm and the sky overhead a radiant blue, a combination guaranteed to elevate the lowest of moods. Even the homeless guy on the corner was whistling a cheerful tune as he aired out his fragrant collection of overcoats on a shopping cart.

I set off on foot, hoping that some fresh air would clear my head and focus my thinking. Or take my mind off my problems altogether. Only when I rounded the corner of my building did I see that the peaks of the mountains north of the city were wearing thick clouds the hue and tensile strength of my grandmother's favourite wig. I sniffed the air, estimating that I had two hours before they arrived to wash away the city's sins. There was little time to waste.

After weaving through the threadbare, have-not carnival along Main Street, I cut through Chinatown. The elegant, inscrutable facades brought Mickey Wu to mind. Business magnates had to be pretty unflappable in stressful situations, but did that include the discovery of corpses in their personal commodes? Aside from what Richard had told me, I realized I didn't really know much more about Mickey Wu than I did about the dead guy. Including whether or not they had been buddies. I hoped that talking to him in person would give me a read on how the corpse cleanup went, and how personally Mickey had taken it.

The warm sunshine and heavy cogitation were resulting in uncomfortable amounts of perspiration on my own corpus. Sensing impending dehydration, I stopped in at the Cambie for a quick pint of the bar's tasteless draft beer, just in case my meeting with Mickey Wu didn't create any headaches of its own.

A familiar cast of local reprobates ebbed and flowed around me according to the workings of their internal, sometimes audible, cuckoo clocks. The guy on the next stool kept asking me to watch his beer while he exited the pub and entered the alley with customers who required stimulants to balance out their depressants. It gave me a pervading sense of calm, knowing that a few of the city's traditional dysfunctions persisted, at least in this part of town. These were degradations on a level I was familiar with, occurring for reasons I understood.

Once sufficiently lubricated, I left the Cambie behind to penetrate the contiguous but disconnected district that was Yaletown. Navigating its cobblestone corridors filled with galleries and brewpubs, I dodged bodybuilders in puffy vests, ladies of leisure walking micro dogs, willowy youth in scarves and blazers carrying their skateboards. It was a diverse and discordant populace drawn together by a shared love of high-end hair product and happy-hour Bellinis.

When I reached False Creek I got in line behind a beefy, fresh-faced family from Minnesota to squeeze onto one of the little bathtub ferries that zigzag up and down the waterway, redistributing tourists according to a secret formula devised by the Vancouver Chamber of Commerce.

The Minnesotans were generating more heat than the sun as they jostled and gawked at the forest of condominiums that lined the shores of False Creek. My canvas jacket was proving far more effective at keeping sweat in than it had ever been at keeping rain out. I managed a passable Houdini impression as I wriggled out of it in the close quarters, the reactivated body funk of the jacket's previous owner permeating the cabin air around me. Dismayed, mouth-breathing Minnesotans edged away from me as I discreetly dropped the jacket to the floor and wedged it under a bench seat with my foot. I made a mental note to stop shopping at the Value Village thrift store on Hastings Street.

Now clad only in my prized powder-blue sateen cowboy shirt with navy accents and pearl snaps, I had no choice but to remain inside as we approached Granville Island. Venturing onto the ferry's tiny outer deck in search of fresher air was to risk getting strafed with the intestinal residue of the seagulls conducting air raids on the untended picnic lunches of the Gore-Tex-clad tourists crowded along the edge of the wharf watching seals picnic on bycatch fish guts.

When the ferryman deposited me at the Maritime Museum in Kitsilano, I made a quick detour up to Siegel's for sesame bagels, delivered hot and fresh straight from the eternal fires of their brick oven. Spiritually and physically fortified, I resumed my journey westward.

By the time I reached Point Grey Road, I was fatigued, footsore, and starting to regret my ambitious perambulations. The clouds were halfway across the harbour, the beer had long since worn off, and I had sesame seeds stuck between my teeth.

Fortunately, my objective was in sight. The bamboo forest surrounding Mickey Wu's house was half a block up, with my car parked on the street in front of it. I had arrived just in time because some nimrod was letting his overgrown pitbull sniff around my car. Only when I got closer did I realize it was actually Mickey Wu and Thaddeus. I chastised myself, recalling that pitbulls seldom wear tracksuits.

"Hello, Mr. Wu." I surveyed the street signs. "I didn't realize this was an off-leash area."

Mickey Wu glanced over. If he was surprised to see me, he didn't show it. "This is your car?" Thaddeus ignored me entirely.

"It sure is." The car was a silver 1983 Porsche 911SC. It wasn't worth much anymore, and I would have been well-advised to drive around with a mechanic if I could have found one small enough to fit in its miniscule trunk. But as far as I was concerned, it was a classic.

Thaddeus continued to circle around it, peering through the windows. I attempted to brush him away with an olive branch. "Like it?" I asked in a not-unfriendly tone.

"No," he grunted, exhaling a moist cloud onto the glass of the passenger window beneath the oily imprint of his forehead pressed against it.

"I was beginning to wonder whether you had abandoned it here," Mickey Wu said.

"Well, I haven't. So if you'll excuse me." I put a hand on Thaddeus' shoulder to pull him away from the car. It was like trying to grab a boulder wrapped in quick-dry polyester.

Mickey Wu watched impassively. "I assume you're here not only to collect your car, but also to return my fee?"

"Of course. Personal cheque alright?"

His eyebrows said "seriously?" but his mouth said, "I suppose."

"Perfect, I just need somewhere to write it out. Shall we go inside? "

Mickey Wu smiled. "Right here is fine."

I decided to do a little fishing while I wrote out the cheque on the hood of my car. "I hope you didn't have much trouble cleaning up after we left?"

"No." Mickey made a show of checking his watch.

"Great." So much for being circumspect. "Did you figure out who the dead guy was?"

"Yes. As a matter fact, I wanted to talk to you about that."

"Oh, yeah?"

Mickey Wu nodded, his expression grim. "It turns out the dead man was the cousin of one of my business associates."

I stopped writing but kept my eyes down, uncertain of what to say. "I had no idea he was a friend of yours. I'm… sorry for your loss?"

"I didn't know him personally, but had been asked to meet with him to see if I could provide him with some… guidance. The man was very troubled. Apparently he had been struggling with addiction for some time. My associate was deeply saddened, if not surprised, to learn that his cousin had overdosed."

I nodded sympathetically. "So I guess it was just bad luck that he showed up the night I was there. No one's fault, really."

Mickey Wu considered this for a moment before replying. "He came to the house looking for me. Instead he stumbled into your party and somehow got his hands on narcotics. Call it bad luck if you wish, but this in no way excuses your own failings."

"Bummer." I elected to ignore the implicit accusation. If Mickey was really hung up on how the guy got the drugs, I'd give him The Norwegian's number. Who, I was relieved to realize, had this whole thing backwards—I hadn't screwed up his business, he had screwed up mine by selling dope to the poor schmuck. "Even though I personally had nothing to do with it, I'm sorry your associate's cousin died." Whoever said apologizing was hard?

"Are you, indeed? Because it seems my associate's tragedy is your good fortune. He has requested that I handle this shameful incident discreetly. I have therefore not contacted the police to report your own negligence and trespasses. In exchange, I expect your absolute discretion. It is, after all, very much in your own interest to keep this matter quiet. Are we agreed on this?"

I nodded, trying not to look too delighted. "I'm just glad we can put this tragic incident behind us now."

Mickey Wu folded his arms across his chest. "Not quite yet, I'm afraid."

I stopped nodding.

"Apparently, some of the man's personal effects have gone missing and the family has asked for my help in recovering them. Naturally I agreed, but we didn't find them when we cleaned up my house." Mickey Wu slipped my cheque into his jacket pocket without looking at it. He was too busy watching me intently. "I was wondering whether you might know where they were."

I tried to look both thoughtful and puzzled. "I'm assuming you aren't referring to the bag of dope that was lying on the bathroom floor?"

Mickey Wu ignored this. "We found the man's wallet, but apparently he also had a cellular phone, which had some content of sentimental value—family photos and the like. They're very keen to recover it."

"Makes sense." Now I actually was puzzled, but attempted to look disinterested. "Wish I could help but I didn't find the phone." Not the one Mickey Wu was describing, at any rate.

He frowned. "You're absolutely sure you didn't find a phone in the bathroom? Or anywhere in my house?"

I shook my head. "Like I said, I wish I could help you."

"What about your friend. Richard, was it? Might he have taken it?"

I felt vicariously offended. "Richard and Dante run a highly professional cleaning service. I assure you that they would never have taken anything from your house."

Despite my indignant assertion, Mickey Wu looked anything but convinced. "I guess we're just going to have to broaden our search."

Unsure of whether he was talking to me or Thaddeus at that point, I said nothing. And neither did he. Mickey Wu simply turned and started up his driveway, with Thaddeus obediently falling into step behind him.

So far, the only thing I had learned was that the dead guy had a family. I hadn't even managed to get inside the house to have a look around. The pressure was building inside me. "Mr. Wu. hold on!"

He glanced back impatiently.

"Any chance I could, uh...use your bathroom?"

Mickey Wu rewarded me with a humourless smile. "Not a chance," he said as he strode away.

I knew I shouldn't have had that second pint.

Chapter Fifteen

I sat in my car and stared out across the ocean toward the North Shore, which had entirely disappeared behind a veil of God's tears. It left me feeling in the dark in more ways than one. The air had become totally still, as if hoping to escape notice, embarrassed by how quickly it had gone from bracing to dank. The thick carpet of grey clouds was gone as well, most likely recalled due to water damage, leaving something that looked like the cement subfloor of the Heavens. The heavy stillness felt at once portentous and peaceful. I always enjoyed the arrival of the west coast winter weather. The problem was it didn't budge for months on end.

I saw from the dashboard clock that I still had a couple hours to kill before Richard finished work—just enough time to take care of some of my own dwindling supply. I flicked on the headlights to illuminate the premature dusk and hit the gas.

I stopped in at three houses, two of which the owners had never set foot in (possibly because corporations don't have feet). The first one didn't even have any furniture, but it did have a bathroom. After making use of it, I did my usual walk-through, changed the position of a few window blinds, checked the appliances, disposed of the junk mail. None of the unoccupied houses owned by my numerous offshore clients were quite as big or fancy as Mickey's, but it occurred to me, belatedly, that they would still have made much better choices for our party. They might even make nice homes for people to live in.

Even after my brief detour into the world of work, I arrived at Dante's condo half an hour early. Located on the north side of False Creek, it was a stylish little fishbowl with an excellent view of the water, as well as a hundred other fishbowls. What made it truly special was that it also had guest parking. I pulled into a spot, shut off the engine, and settled in to listen to the pitter patter of little feet as the raindrops ran down my windshield. I was just starting to doze off when Richard rapped on the driver's side window, looking worried but dry beneath the blue and white sprawl of a Palm Springs Hilton golf umbrella.

"So I guess you haven't heard from him?" I locked the car with the key. Classics do have their inconveniences.

He shook his head and hurried toward the building with me right behind him, chasing after the unused real estate beneath his gargantuan umbrella. "Not a word. It's not like I expect him to report in all the time, but still."

"Relationship Commandment Number 5," I said supportively.

"He's played hooky from work a couple times before—we both have. But we've always texted each other when we do to make sure at least one of us shows up for the job." He glanced over his shoulder at me. "And finding his condo broken into? That totally freaked me out."

After Richard convinced the keypad to unlock the front door of the building for us, we waited for the elevator in silence since I had nothing new or comforting to share. We rode it up to the seventh floor, got off and headed down the hall. I heard Richard suck in his breath as we rounded the corner. Looking past him, I saw Dante's door hanging open.

"I closed the door when I left," said Richard excitedly. "He must be back!"

Before I could reply, he raced ahead and disappeared into the condo calling Dante's name. I ran after him. As soon as I was through the doorway, my rib cage short circuited. Or at least that's what it felt like when a jolt of pain on the right side of my chest sent me reeling. I bounced off the wall and lost my footing in the tangle of coats on the floor in front of the hall closet, ending up flat on my back.

I opened my eyes and turned my head to see a pair of day-glo Nikes mere inches from my face. "Oh, shit," said a female voice.

I looked up to identify their owner. "Wii...mindy?" I attempted a smile, but grimaced instead as an aftershock coursed through my body.

She frowned down at me. "Say what?"

Richard reappeared in the doorway of Dante's bedroom across the hall. "Wendy! What did you do, girl?"

"Richard! I'm so glad it's you. I was in the kitchen when I heard someone come charging through the door. I got back just in time to zap him." She gestured toward me with a small black device that resembled my TV remote control. The main differences being that this one wasn't at the bottom of my aquarium, and obviously it still worked.

"Sorry about that, by the way," she added before looking back at Richard. "Where's Dante? His door was busted open and the whole place is a mess. I was just about to call the cops."

"I don't know where he is. I'm totally worried. Some pretty weird stuff is going on." Richard waved his hands in frustration. "I don't even know where to start."

I lay on the floor trying to breathe while I listened to Richard bring Wendy up to speed on the post-party break-ins. From their discussion, I learned that she was Dante's upstairs neighbour and a good friend. Wendy was also a sales rep for a nutritional supplements company and had stopped in to drop off Dante's latest order.

"Hold on," I cut in. "So that actually was Vitamin C you gave me at the party?"

Wendy stopped talking to Richard long enough to frown at me again. "How many fingers am I holding up?" She flashed me a peace sign.

"Two. Why?"

"I was worried I might have scrambled your brains with my stun gun. No, of course that wasn't Vitamin C! It was E, as in Ecstasy. And you owe me thirty bucks, by the way."

I frowned back at her. "That seems a little steep."

She snorted. "Those tabs were pure, man. You wanna pay ten bucks and get spiked with fentanyl, go ahead. But you're not going to get that shit from me."

"Okay, okay. No need to get pissy about it." I took the high road and dug into my pocket for my wallet as I stood up. Customer service had never been my strong suit either, and there was no disputing the quality of Wendy's product.

"Do you mind?" Richard cut in testily. "If you two are finished talking business, can we get back to Dante?"

Chapter Sixteen

Dante's condo had been thoroughly searched, but as far as Richard could tell, little was missing, same as ours. In the hallway by the front door, a table had been smashed and there was a dent in the drywall, which Richard was convinced was exactly the size and altitude of Dante's head. And of course the door had been forced open.

"So tell me again why you think a Norwegian did this," Wendy said.

"Not *a* Norwegian, *The* Norwegian. He did it because he's a drug dealer and a thug. As well as Jake's ex business partner," Richard said testily.

Wendy raised her eyebrows. "Putting aside Jake's business acumen for a moment, I still don't get why this Norwegian guy would come after Dante."

"As payback for Jake messing up The Norwegian's business the other night."

"Which he did by having a party?"

Richard folded his arms across his chest. "Exactly."

"That makes no sense. How could having a party mess up his business? Drug dealers love parties." Wendy took another sip of the excellent Rioja she had convinced Richard to pilfer from Dante's wine rack. We thought it would calm him down to have a drink. Instead, he gulped down three and was now even more worked up than before.

"Ask Jake," Richard snapped.

Wendy looked over at me. "How could having a party mess up a drug dealer's business?"

"No idea. But that's beside the point anyway. If he's going to punish anyone for screwing up his business, it'll be me. The Norwegian barely knows Dante—he thought his name was Donny." I grinned at Richard, hoping he might find a bit of humour in this, but he avoided my gaze.

I tried again. "He barely knows Dante, right?"

Richard said nothing and reached for the wine bottle. Finding it empty, he got up and disappeared into the kitchen.

"So whose house did you have that party in, anyway?" Wendy asked while we waited for Richard to reappear.

I put my hand on my chest. "Why do you assume it wasn't mine?"

"Multimillionaires tend to have matching shoelaces."

This sounded plausible so I decided to let it pass. "The place belongs to a guy I work for. Or used to, anyway. A Chinese thong magnate named Mickey Wu."

Wendy contemplated this for a moment. "So you're big into thongs?"

"What? No." It took me a minute to get my mind back on track. "I worked for him as a house-sitter. Not selling underwear."

"Ah, so you don't just sit on them, but provide house-warming services as well. That's a full-service operation you're running."

I studied her closely to be sure. She was definitely smirking. I went with it. "That's right. And for a rather exclusive client list, I might add. But after this weekend, an opening has come up, so let me know if you're interested."

"I just might be," she replied with a full blown smile.

"Oh, yeah?" I sounded more surprised than I intended. Before I could improve my response, Richard came back into the room.

"Nothing left but this Chardonnay," he announced, sloshing some into his glass, heedless of the Rioja dregs. The result was an unappetizing rosé. Not that there was any other kind. "So. Where were we?"

"I commented that The Norwegian barely knows Dante, and you got squirrelly and left the room."

Richard stared into his glass for a minute and then sighed. "The Norwegian knows Dante a lot better than you think."

I drained the rest of my wine and swallowed a couple more times for good measure before asking the question. "How?"

"Before I met him, Dante used to be quite a partier. Nothing too crazy, but he liked to do a bit of coke here and there." Richard shifted uncomfortably in his seat. "When you cut The Norwegian's pot supply, he moved into coke and Dante started buying from him."

I was too surprised to reply immediately. When I did, it landed slightly beside the point. "I thought Dante didn't even drink."

"He doesn't. All those empty calories. A moment on the lips, right?" Richard shrugged. "But he enjoys coke."

I couldn't believe that all this time Dante had been buying it from The Norwegian. I thought they had met only once, buying a half-ounce back when The Norwegian and I were working together.

Wendy shrugged. "So he's a valued customer of The Norwegian's. All the more reason that he wouldn't come after Dante."

Richard raised his glass to take another drink and then stopped and frowned at it uncertainly. "As far as I know, Dante hasn't bought anything from The Norwegian in almost a year. The last time he did, things didn't go so well."

"What happened?" asked Wendy.

"Dante made fun of The Norwegian's trench coat."

I put my head in my hands and let out a groan.

Wendy looked back and forth between us impatiently. "So what?"

"Let's just say the man has a very thin skin. Which he protects with his prized pterodactyl-skin coat." Richard looked queasy. "Why did you ever get involved with the man, Jake? He's a Neanderthal."

I felt a surge of annoyance. "It was a bad choice, I freely admit it. That's why I parted ways with him years ago. Which is more than I can say for Dante. Since you knew what a thug he was, why the hell did you let Dante buy coke from him?" I felt like a jerk even before I had finished saying the words. Dante was missing, most likely in danger, and Richard was convinced that The Norwegian was involved. He was probably feeling guilty enough already.

"Fuck you! I didn't *let* Dante do anything. He's a grown man, not my ward!"

Or possibly angry. I remembered Relationship Commandment Number 1: Do What You Feel. Richard had stolen this one from Omar Little after watching *The Wire*, but that didn't make it any less true.

"Boys, boys." Wendy raised her hands in a placating gesture. "Enough bickering. It's getting late and I haven't even had dinner or changed out of this monkey suit I wear to work." She tugged at her yoga pants with visible annoyance. "So can we focus on Dante and decide what we're going to do about finding him?"

I nodded, thankful for her interjection. The yoga pants were just a work uniform, not a preferred fashion. I had been worried she liked them as much as they liked her. "It's dangerous to make fun of The Norwegian's sartorial quirks, but if it's any comfort, in my experience his vengeance tends more toward 'swift and terrible' than 'best served cold.' I really doubt he would've waited a year to come after Dante."

"Unless he happened to be looking for a way to get back

at you as well," Richard countered. "He did say he had to punish you for messing with his business, and he knows we're close friends."

I could feel Richard and Wendy's eyes upon me as I chewed my lip. It still didn't feel right to me, but I had to admit it wasn't as thin as my Lazy Burglar theory had been. "So what do you want to do?"

"Call the cops." Richard gestured around the condo. "Look at this place."

I sighed. "Okay. Go ahead. But first, let me fill you in on what Mickey Wu told me so we can get our stories straight on the party and the dead guy."

Wendy looked over at me. "Dead guy?"

Chapter Seventeen

While we were waiting for the cops to show up, it dawned on us that they probably wouldn't be too impressed to find us lounging around drinking wine in the middle of a crime scene. Fortunately, Wendy lived directly above it.

She led the way up the building's fire stairs. Richard followed behind her, blocking my view with his own glutei maximi. I wanted to avert my eyes, but would've had as much luck trying not to watch Brad Pitt on the big screen.

She opened her door and ushered us into the lounge before disappearing into her bedroom to change. Her unit was a cookie-cutter reproduction of Dante's, and a whole different world. His was a zen garden; hers an owl's nest. When at Dante's, I was inclined, more often than not, to speak in hushed tones. Wendy's made me want to shout and jump around. Both were temples for, and testaments to, master craftspeople carrying on ancient traditions.

Richard had seen it all before. He busied himself with ordering Thai food. The police officer he talked to while still at Dante's had told him that a missing person was not an emergency so it would probably be a couple hours before they could spare anyone.

While Richard was on his phone, mine buzzed at me. Speak of the devil and he doth text:

> got you voice-mail. I have what your looking
> for. If you want back meet me tomorrow night

The typos were understandable. The Norwegian had fingers the size of bratwurst. Knowing Richard was going to freak out when I showed him the text, I felt it best to wait until he had finished ordering dinner.

My Thai was non-existent even when not compared to his fluency, so I was left to assume that the process was complete when he terminated the call. I bit the bullet and swallowed twice. "Richard…" I began.

He held up a finger. "Hold on. Voice-mail."

I watched his face perform a rather compelling medley of emotive contortions, from concentration to relief, followed by surprise, and then an electrifying swan song of excitement mixed with petulance. "Dante's okay!" he exclaimed. "And I'm going to kill him."

Wendy came hurrying down the hallway. She had changed into a pair of faded brown corduroys and a green t-shirt with a chimpanzee wearing glasses and a suit with the caption '98% you,' which inspired a mix of excitement and petulance in me. For one thing, I didn't even own a suit.

Richard beamed at us. "I just got a message from Dante. That bitch is on a freaking yacht right now."

Wendy clapped her hands. "Whose yacht?"

"Chip Thompson's." Richard laughed and shook his head.

"Chip Thompson? As in, *the* Chip Thompson? The guy who invented *Near Future*?" Wendy's eyes were as wide and green as a pair of lost lagoons.

Richard switched to nodding his head. "Him. Maybe Dante never mentioned he's an ex?"

"He did not. That bitch." Wendy grinned.

I felt compelled to pull back on the conversational reins. "Hold up a minute. Who the hell is Chip Thompson?"

The incredulity in their expressions came across as a pretty heavy load of judgment for posing an innocent question.

"That kid who created the *Near Future* computer game? Who's now, like, what, a bazillionaire?" Wendy finished off by shaking her head in slow motion.

"He's not a kid," Richard amended in a huffy tone.

"He runs a gaming company down in San Francisco, doesn't he?" Wendy said.

Richard nodded. "But he's originally from Vancouver. Dante dated him for a few months before we got together. Chip was living in his parents' basement at the time, working on the game, I guess. When he wasn't writing code, he was checking out online hookup sites." Richard skillfully executed a lewd finger mamba by way of illustration. "They hooked up. But Dante dumped him pretty quickly. According to him, Chip was marooned in arrested adolescence. I believe his exact words were 'total failure to launch.'"

Wendy laughed. "Kinda seems like he launched after all."

"Tell me about it. I used to tease Dante about it but he brushed it off, claiming he didn't care about the money. He said Chip was an obsessive little megalomaniac who was more interested in video games than sex."

"So what's he doing on the guy's boat?" I hoped to squeeze some relevance out of the conversation. It all sounded like good news, but I was having trouble reconciling it with The Norwegian's text. If he didn't have Dante, then who, or what, did he think I was looking for? I decided to puzzle that one out on my own as I didn't want to spoil Richard's good mood by bringing up The Norwegian again.

"Chip called him from his yacht last night, told him he was coming into town." Richard shook his head. "Who knows? Maybe he's trying to rub Dante's face in his success, show off a little. And like I said, Dante loves to party. They've been sailing through the Gulf Islands but they're coming in for supplies tomorrow morning and…" He paused to do a little dance. "Dante got Chip to agree to let me come along for the second half of their party cruise!"

"Now you're the bitch!" Wendy laughed.

Richard giggled and thrust his hands into the air in a victorious gesture.

"But wait, if Dante just went yachting with the digerati, then who broke into his place?" Wendy asked. "And yours?"

Richard put his hands on his hips. "My money's still on The Norwegian, punishing us because he thinks we messed things up for him somehow. The important thing is that Dante's okay, and I'm going sailing!"

"What about the cops?" Wendy asked.

A rogue wave of panic rolled across Richard's features. "Oh, shit. I better call them off. And call Dante back. Can I use your bedroom, Wen?"

She nodded and jerked her thumb toward the hallway. After Richard left, Wendy flopped down beside me on the sofa. She propped herself up with an elbow and begun to study me with a faintly amused expression when the front door banged opened.

A woman in her thirties walked in. She was wearing a blue bomber jacket over a blue button-up shirt, which merged in an orderly fashion with blue cargo pants. Her manner of speech was as efficient as her dress: "Hey, Wen," she said, kneeling down to untie heavy black boots. I bet everything on a pair of black socks but lost it all. They were white. Her hair was blond, and heavily shellacked, seemingly for optimal aerodynamics. When she stood up and saw me, she frowned and added a terse hello.

"Hey," Wendy replied without looking over.

"I'm going to take a shower," the woman announced.

"Okay."

"Who's that?" I asked after she marched off down the hall.

"Barb," Wendy replied. "We live together."

Richard's reappearance saved me from languishing in disappointment. "The cops aren't coming," he announced.

"Did you talk to Dante?" Wendy asked, looking over at him.

"No, his phone went straight to voice-mail."

"Well, like you said, the important thing is that he's okay. And you'll see your man tomorrow," Wendy reminded him sympathetically.

Richard sighed and looked out the window.

Sensing that things were getting mopey, I waded in. "Who wants to hear what I found out about the dead guy?"

After telling Wendy about our mysterious party guest's untimely demise and Mickey Wu's untimely return, I filled them in on what he had told me about his business associate, and that the dead guy's family was trying to locate his missing phone. By the time I was done, Richard looked distracted, but Wendy was nodding.

"Sounds like you got served a big, fat baloney sandwich," she said.

I nodded back at her glumly. If the story had sounded any more convincing to them, I probably could've talked myself into believing it and forgetting that the whole sordid weekend ever happened.

Richard seemed to have the same idea now that Dante's whereabouts were no longer in question. He announced that he was going home to look for something "yachty" to wear.

My initial inclination to linger and talk vitamins with Wendy was kiboshed by Barb's reappearance, throwing off wafts of lilac and wearing yoga pants identical to the ones Wendy had recently shed. Barb busied herself in the kitchen preparing some kind of foul-smelling lentil stew and setting the table. Noisily, and with only two bowls.

I took the hint and hit the road.

Chapter Eighteen

I was starting to feel pretty positive about how things were sorting themselves out. What had started out as a possible murder and a missing friend was now down to a rash of break-ins in a city where property crime rates were on the rise, purportedly due to the scourge of illegal drug use. If that was all that was going on, it was the kind of karmic retribution I was prepared to endure.

My newfound optimism ticked up a notch when I arrived home to discover that the quality of my uninvited guests had improved. In marked contrast to The Norwegian, this one was waiting, albeit impatiently, on my doorstep, and actually looked good in leather pants. I invited her inside.

"Why didn't you call me back?" Nina asked.

"I did. I just didn't leave a message."

She frowned distractedly.

"You never check them anyway." I immediately resented myself for defending myself.

"I always check my messages."

"Even the ones from me?" It was like I never learned.

Nina hid the truth behind a sultry smile. "I don't have to. I already know what you want."

Feeling magnanimous and a bit horny, I chose to overlook the patronizing subtext and focus on the smile. "Is that why you dropped by so late?"

Smile, I barely knew you. Nina, on the other hand, I knew all too well. She switched to teasing my tetras by tapping her fingers on the aquarium glass. I consoled myself with three fingers of a different kind. Once the Woodford Reserve was in the glass, I dropped my butt into the Eames chair and waited.

"You really screwed things up for me with your stupid party, Constable."

Nina and The Norwegian had more in common than I would have guessed. "How so? The other day you said it wasn't a problem. That Mickey Wu was a nobody."

She turned and pinned me to the chair with an expression of recrimination that was familiar, but at the same time utterly alien in its vulnerability. "If that's true, then why did two men from the Chinese government show up at my office to interrogate me?"

I paused for a fortifying gulp of bourbon. "What did they want?" I already knew the answer.

Nina shrugged unhappily. "All sorts of weird stuff—How well did I know Mickey Wu? Is he a Canadian citizen? Who does he associate with?"

"What did you tell them?" I suspected I knew the answer to this one as well.

She averted her gaze. Her eyes began darting in unison with the movements of the fish. "What could I tell them? I have no idea whether he's a Canadian citizen."

"Or who he associates with?"

Nina didn't say anything.

"Did you really have to tell those guys that I was a drug dealer?"

Nina shook her head quickly, her eyes those of a freshly slain doe. "I said that you used to be, not that you are."

"Guess they weren't taking very good notes."

Nina turned her back on the fish. "You should be thanking me, anyway."

"How do you figure that?"

"Because I didn't tell them about what happened at your stupid party."

It was refreshing for Nina to say something I didn't immediately want to argue with. "But why did you have to tell them anything? Those guys admitted they have no jurisdiction here, no official powers."

"I'm sorry, Jake. I got spooked, okay? I just needed to tell them something so they would go away and leave me alone. You have no idea how these people operate. The kind of pressure they can bring to bear."

"But you haven't done anything wrong. And you're a Canadian citizen. What kind of pressure can they put on you?"

"Not me. My uncle."

"But you said he wasn't worried about Mickey Wu. That he was a nobody."

Nina nodded at the tetras.

"So what's the problem?"

"My uncle has been investigated by the Chinese government in the past."

"I thought your uncle *was* the Chinese government. Didn't you tell me he was some kind of power broker on the Central Committee?"

"He used to be. But not right now. We're hoping he will be reappointed. But like all powerful men, he has enemies. And competitors. So if he's linked to anything scandalous…"

"Like a snuff party?" Even I could imagine the political landmine my party could become in the hands of a decent spin doctor. It was enough to make a lesser man feel guilty.

Nina nodded. "You didn't tell them anything about that, did you?"

"Of course not. But are these guys investigating Mickey Wu or your uncle?"

"I don't know."

"Shouldn't you at least tell your uncle that they came nosing around?"

"I don't know."

In that moment, Nina looked scared and out of her depth. Providing comfort and assistance in such moments was not something I knew anything about because there had never been any during our time together. "What can I do?"

"I don't know."

At least I gave it a shot. "I'm going to bed." I gave the tetras a pinch of dinner and left the room.

Nina had proven long ago that she was capable of finding her own way to my bedroom. And the front door.

Chapter Nineteen

I woke up alone, and not all that unhappy about it. Catching up on my sleep had been only a little further down my "to do" list than the other thing.

The living room was empty but the Eames chair still bore Nina's scent, if not her warmth. I briefly rifled the memory bank for a mental image of her curled up in it but came up 404. The neon tetras didn't say how long she stayed and I didn't ask. Respect for each other's privacy was one of the reasons the fish and I got along so well. I sprinkled a pinch of stinky flakes into their water and vacated the premises.

After a leisurely breakfast with George, I joined a fragrant parade of middle-aged men with nothing better to do than hang out in the public library and read old newspapers. I hadn't been able to recall any cozy domestic scenes with Nina, but her anxiety about the government investigators had conjured up something else from my sepia-toned memories of our time together.

It was right at the beginning of things, when each moment still felt unpredictable and indelible. Most of the details of this particular morning had now faded into obscurity, but I recalled mimosas, homemade waffles with ice cream and syrup, a swapping (yes, a swapping) of t-shirts retrieved from beside the sofa where they had been discarded hours earlier, and the *New York Times*. It was January. Later in the month, if my visual and olfactory recollections of the desiccated state of Nina's Christmas tree were to be trusted.

Waffles demolished, I was working hard at looking like I wasn't working hard on the crossword, but "bird of prey with a woman's face," five letters, had me at sixes and sevens. Nina hadn't noticed. She was engrossed by an article about China in the paper. Something about its potential impact on her family and her business had set her on edge. I nodded solemnly and made sympathetic noises, all the while trying to name the elusive creature.

If only I had paid more attention to Nina when it mattered, truly listened to her. Maybe I wouldn't be alone now, crammed into a carrel covered with grammatically-suspect graffiti and the odd sticky patch, waiting for a man wearing two hats and orange striped pajama pants to finish reading the obituaries in a four-year-old newspaper.

Nina subscribed to the Sunday edition of the *Times*, which narrowed my search down to four papers. Each one the size and word count of a complete set of the Encyclopaedia Britannica. I made it through the first two by lunch but nothing jumped out at me. After three dollar slices of pizza (two Hawaiian, one pesto), I perused the third.

When I returned from an espresso break, the fourth issue was nowhere to be found. After bothering the denizens of the study carrels long enough to have to explain myself to the periodicals clerk, I finally spotted it, pinned to a communal reading table beneath the virulent outposts of psoriasis that were Mr. Two Hats' elbows.

For three-quarters of an hour, I watched as he alternately frowned at, napped on, and scribbled in the newspaper I needed. I finally paid him ten dollars for it. After another three-quarters of an hour, I deemed it money well-spent. It wasn't difficult to narrow down the possibilities since only five articles in the paper mentioned China.

One profiled a panda at the Beijing Zoo named Ling-Ling, who delighted visitors by repeatedly hugging a zookeeper's legs. Nina wasn't what you'd call an animal lover, but I nevertheless felt confident this wasn't the article that had vexed her. Two articles focused on China's attempts to outmaneuver its neighbours in claiming portions of the South China Sea. I dismissed those as well since Nina had even less time for politics than animals.

Which left two articles, companion pieces. One discussed the diaspora of wealthy Chinese expats, many of whom were former state officials, buying up luxury real estate throughout North America. This must have been newsworthy at the time, but it was a state of affairs that has been commonplace in Vancouver for years now. I moved on to the next article.

The second article described the Chinese government's attempts to not only stem this outflow of citizens and currency, but to reverse it. Primarily through a quasi-covert initiative called Operation Fox Hunt. There was an unattributed quote from a U.S. government representative stating that Uncle Sam was Officially Pissed Off that Chinese agents were sneaking around trying to strong-arm rich expats into returning home, but the article was otherwise short on details. I found it an enjoyable read nonetheless for having successfully walked a suggestive line between hard news and conspiracy theory. What it didn't bother to do was paint the targets of Operation Fox Hunt as "little guy" victims of government oppression (I read the phrase "robber barons" more than once in between-the-lines font).

After finishing the articles, I relocated to one of the library's computers and did an Internet search on Operation Fox Hunt. Most of the stories I found online didn't so much walk the line between hard news and conspiracy theory as trample it into oblivion. After filtering out some of the more sensationalistic cloak-and-dagger allegations, I was left with

descriptions of two tried-and-true techniques employed by the
Fox Hunters. The first was nailing the expat for one of their
crimes back home, which were apparently legion. This actually sounded more difficult than I would have expected, due
to a lack of extradition treaties combined with an enervating
web of jurisdictional issues in which the globetrotting expats
attempted to entangle themselves. One website described
how the mastermind of a billion-dollar smuggling ring in
China submitted multiple claims for refugee status in order
to remain in Canada for years. The claims were ultimately
rejected, possibly undermined by his habit of going on month-
long, multimillion-dollar casino gambling sprees and getting
chauffeured around in a ninety-thousand-dollar SUV.

The second approach appeared to be the Chinese government's response to all the judicial red tape. It was alleged that
pressure was applied on the expats indirectly, via vulnerable
family members. According to sources who wished to remain
anonymous, any family members the expat had in China were
at risk of incarceration (inevitably on "trumped-up charges"),
while those living abroad were subject to harassment. There
were even a couple reports of people disappearing from various locations only to reappear back in China as loyal and
obedient citizens.

Having reached the limits of my research skills and patience,
I turned my attention back to the *New York Times* with the
hope of resolving the other outstanding issue from that cold
day in January. In doing so, I also discovered the reason for
Mr. Two Hats' feverish scribbling. I looked up and scanned
the library, but he was gone. I would never have the chance
to apologize for underestimating the man. Forty-five minutes
wasn't close to record time for completing the Sunday crossword, but it was still impressive. Particularly if you factored
in the naps.

The clue that I should have gotten four years earlier was
"harpy."

Chapter Twenty

Things started out well. The Norwegian arrived just after nine p.m., knocking on my door rather than kicking it off the hinges. The presentation of my mason jar, empty but intact, bordered on ceremonious. "Like I texted. You were looking for this, yes? I confiscated it as punishment for screwing me up with your party." He patted me on the shoulder. "Very good weed, Constable. You haven't lost your touch."

"Glad you liked it. Come on in and make yourself comfortable—on the sofa. Want a beer?" I knew I could use one. A house call from The Norwegian was categorically not a good thing.

He shook his head. "Get your coat. We're going for a drive. I want to show you something."

With him being so cordial, it seemed impolite, definitely unhealthy, to argue. I got my coat.

We didn't talk on the way. Not because I didn't have questions in need of answers, but because I couldn't scream as loudly as the lead singer of Dimmu Borgir—a symphonic black metal band from Oslo that, judging from his serene smile, sated The Norwegian's patriotic and/or primal requirements. I found myself pining for Dante's Gregorian chants.

Although The Norwegian enjoyed working with his hands, he was no handyman. Which is why I had never understood his choice of vehicle—a shiny, black, crew cab pickup truck with oversized, dual wheels in the rear and heavy-duty suspension that made the thing ride like a buckboard. It was almost as excruciating as the noise coming from under the hood, which sounded like gravel being fed through a sausage grinder. The Norwegian had to crank the truck's stereo to full volume to compete with the roar of what must've been an enormous diesel engine. Or Satan, chained up under the hood receiving a motor oil enema while singing backup for Dimmu Borgir.

The resulting cacophony overwhelmed all thought, including the second ones I would have otherwise had when The Norwegian left busy, well-lit South Granville Street and turned into a quiet, dark alley. After another half block, he nosed the truck into a makeshift driveway, basically a collapsed section of fence, behind a ramshackle bungalow with peeling paint and blacked-out windows.

After he turned off the ignition in the truck, I could still hear the traffic on Granville Street, only a couple hundred metres distant, but at the same time a world away. The only signs of life in the immediate vicinity came from the family of raccoons cowering beneath the steps leading up to the back door of the house. When we approached, they chittered at us indignantly before scuttling off to disappear over the fence of the similarly derelict house next door.

Inside, I was greeted by empty rooms and a dry, musty smell suggestive of windows and doors that seldom stayed opened for long. When The Norwegian closed the door behind me, the comforting drone of traffic went silent. It was replaced by a faint electrical hum from the basement. Which is where The Norwegian took me.

At the bottom of the stairs, he pushed aside a heavy velvet curtain that looked like it had been stolen from the Rialto movie theatre around the time talkies were becoming popular.

We were instantly bathed in bright light. Temporarily blinded, I heard the crinkle plastic and felt it brush against me as I followed my ex-business partner into the basement.

Heat and humidity closed in on me, causing a sheen of sweat to spring up on my forehead even before The Norwegian started questioning me.

"Why did you lie to me the other night, Constable?"

"Are you serious? You know I'd never be stupid enough to lie to you." I heard the nervousness in my voice, even though I was telling the truth. To calm myself, I inhaled deeply, taking in the cloying fragrance of the rows of marijuana plants that surrounded us. The glare of the hydroponic lights added an undeniable sense of drama to The Norwegian's interrogation. As did the six millimetre plastic sheeting I was standing on, the kind used to create vapour barriers in walls. Or airtight enclosures around grow ops in basements.

The third use that came to mind was the one that was throwing me—containing the mess made by assassins in Hollywood movies. I couldn't get the image of the victim standing on the plastic sheet while the killer screwed the silencer onto his pistol.

I stopped admiring the forest of buds long enough to risk a quick glance at The Norwegian, relieved to see that his hands were empty. Less comforting was the fact that they were clenched into fists the size and abrasiveness of cinder blocks.

I resumed my inspection of the grow op since the hydroponics were throwing off less heat than The Norwegian's scowl. Exclusively an outside grower, I didn't claim to be any kind of expert but was nevertheless impressed by his setup. Stud framing had been erected around the plants, with plastic sheeting stapled on and seam-sealed with Tuck Tape. Rows of hydroponics and a powerful ventilation system hummed within it. When we came into the house, my knowledgeable nose hadn't even suspected the existence of a thriving indoor jungle in the basement.

No doubt about it, The Norwegian could really hide evidence of criminal activities with a few metres of poly sheeting and some tape. I wasn't thrilled to see leftover rolls of both lying in the corner.

"If you're not back in the business, then why did my supplier mention your name?" he rumbled.

"I have no idea. I don't even know who your supplier is." I racked my brains before The Norwegian did it for me. "I did, uh…bump into Martin Farrell recently. He seemed pretty up to speed on your connects these days. Maybe Martin mentioned me to your supplier?" If someone had to go under the bus, I figured it might as well be the guy who feels no pain. Plus, I knew The Norwegian had far too good a head for business to rough-up a cash cow like Martin.

The Norwegian looked unconvinced. "No way Farrell would ever get near my supplier."

I took a small step backwards only because there wasn't enough room to take a big one. My heel hit a 2x4 offcut from the grow op's framing. Out of the corner of my eye I saw The Norwegian smile as I maneuvered into position to grab it.

"Calm down, Constable. I'm not going to hurt you. The boss can bring in more than enough product for both of us, but I need to know what your angle is."

I threw my hands up in frustration, if not surrender. I got into enough trouble for the things I actually did, and horning in on The Norwegian's business definitely wasn't one of them. I had no idea how to convince him I didn't know or care who he was dealing for, but I knew I had to try. "Was your supplier around, back when you and I were working together? Because we did have quite the rep for top-quality product. Maybe he remembered me and figured if we worked on this grow op together, we could… "

"This?" The Norwegian cut me off with a dismissive gesture. "This is just to pay a few mortgages." A wave of childlike enthusiasm thawed his facial fjords. "Come with me."

I wasted no time in following The Norwegian up the stairs and back out onto the porch.

"What do you see?" he asked.

"A chronic lack of lawn care." Glowing white eyes watched us through the slats in the fence. "Raccoons."

"Wrong."

I studied the shapes in the darkness. They were definitely raccoons but it seemed unwise to argue the point. "Okay then, what do I see?"

"Condos," he proclaimed with an obstinacy birthed by ancient and obscure Norse gods. "What do you think the population of Vancouver will be fifteen years from now?"

I shrugged. Somewhere between the six-mil poly sheeting and the imaginary condos, I had gotten completely lost.

"More than three million people! Where do you think they're going to live?"

The Norwegian saved me the trouble of shrugging a second time. He stomped down on the porch with enough force to crack one of the half-rotten boards beneath our feet. "Right here."

On the other side of the fence, four sets of eyes widened in alarm before winking out entirely.

"There, too." He nodded toward the neighbouring house. "I own them both," he announced proudly.

"Impressive," I admitted. Now for the delicate part. "Did you, uh, set up two grow ops right beside each other? I assume you're running them off meter, but BC Hydro still might notice the spike in power-consumption."

"I'm not an amateur, Constable. The other house, I just use for… storage. And this is my last grow show, anyway. I can't afford to go back to jail."

"You're an ex-con? You never told me that." I hadn't asked for his résumé when we went into business together, but it still seemed like the kind of thing he should've told me.

"It was after you quit on me. I was handling some collections work that went wrong, ended up doing a couple years for aggravated assault."

I made an "ouch" face. "Sorry to hear it."

He waved off my attempt at commiseration. "It was actually really good for me."

"How so?" I immediately regretted my question. The last thing I wanted to hear was some hokey inspirational tale of how he had found Thor.

"I was expecting a murder rap but it turned out the guy was only in a coma." Before I could dodge it, one of his elbows buried itself in my rib cage. "What do you think happened?" He tried to suppress a grin.

"He woke up?" I wheezed.

The Norwegian chortled with delight. "Yes! Sloppy work on my part, but also lucky—my lawyer says if I get sent up for anything like that again, I'll be growing old in there. So that's that; I'm going legit. No more rough stuff. I'm even getting out of the drug biz."

I waited for the punch line but none came. "What about the, uh…incident in the bathroom at the party? That *was* you, wasn't it?"

The Norwegian looked surprised. "You know about that, eh? The guy got what was coming to him, that's all."

"But you just said you were done roughing people up." Judging by The Norwegian's growing irritation, it seemed an opportune time to remind him of this.

"What's your point?"

"So you didn't, uh…kill the guy?"

"What? No, I didn't kill him!" The Norwegian's leather coat protested audibly as he crossed his arms. "What's with all these questions? Do I need to pat you down for a wire?"

I raised my arms. "Go ahead."

The Norwegian studied me for a moment before gesturing

dismissively. "It was just a blackmail thing I was handling as a favour for the boss."

This took me by surprise. "Blackmail? Not dope?" I assumed the bag of powder we found beside the dead guy had been sold to him by The Norwegian, but maybe I was wrong and he was telling me the truth about getting out of the drug game.

The Norwegian shrugged. "Obviously, I'm moving some product too. But that's mostly to capitalize my new business."

Nope, not wrong, after all. Same old Norwegian. I allowed myself a small smile, which he mistook for enthusiasm.

"Want to know what it is?"

I totally did not. "Sure."

"Property development! Guess how much cash has been moved out of China over the past eighteen months."

I shrugged. "Millions?"

His booming laugh started a dog barking a few houses over. "Try billions! With most of it going straight into North American real estate. The Chinese government won't admit it, but their economy has slowed significantly and there is growing risk of currency devaluation. Plus, they limit the amount of cash that citizens are allowed to transfer out of the country. Real estate investments are a secure way to move money around while maintaining adequate liquidity."

I recognized his tone of voice, if not the terminology. The Norwegian had switched into MBA seminar mode, and asset diversification had always been one of his favourite topics. "So you're going to get a piece of the action?" I interjected, hoping to foreclose on the property spiel.

He laid a heavy hand on my shoulder. "And you're going to help me do it."

"Me? But I don't know anything about property development."

The Norwegian grinned. "But you do know a good realtor."

Chapter Twenty-one

The meeting with The Norwegian turned out to be a decidedly mixed bag. In the win column, I suffered no bodily harm. On the other side of the ledger, the prospect of us going back into business together was a profoundly daunting turn of events. Especially since it now seemed to comprise drugs, blackmail, and property development—a sleazier trifecta I couldn't begin to imagine.

Even more daunting was the prospect of telling Nina that The Norwegian wanted her to be his real estate agent. I would have to find a way to extricate both of us, but it was after midnight by the time I got back to my place, so at least it wasn't something I had to face immediately. I decided to start bright and early the next day with the easier task of tracking down an opium kingpin to prove to The Norwegian that I wasn't one of his dealers.

Having settled on a plan of action, I washed away my residual nerves with a slug of Cazadores tequila and went to bed.

• • ● • •

The city sanitation department's diesel-powered alarm woke me at eight a.m. An unforgivably late hour for the markets. Unless you're talking about those dealing in narcotics, in which case it was ungodly early. I killed some time showering and caffeinating before heading off on my search.

The air along Hastings Street was grey and hazy, as if the sun was neglecting the street like everyone else. Or maybe it knew it wouldn't be doing anyone any favours by warming up whatever biomass was emitting the various fetid odours wafting from the alleyways. The scant daylight caused me to make a rookie mistake and forget my sunglasses. To avoid making eye contact with the street preachers and screechers, I studied the overhead signs of the long-stay hotels, conjoined bars, and cheque-cashing stores that accounted for the bulk of retail services available in the neighbourhood. A listless drizzle was falling by the time I reached my destination, half a block past the jovial neon pig that presided over the entrance to Save-On-Meats.

The Hyundai was still there, now sporting a few new parking tickets and a set of wheel locks, but Martin was nowhere to be found. After waiting in the rain long enough to be offered skunk weed, crack, and a free personality test at the Church of Scientology, I gave up and went into the Easy Mart for some breakfast.

I placed the Twix bar on the counter, wincing as the fluorescent lights reflected off the cashier's scalp, ill-concealed beneath the suggestion of a pompadour sculpted out of oiled strands of hair laboriously harvested from the back of his skull. The man was unquestionably a maestro with a comb, but the raw materials were sorely lacking.

"Pay for the coffee already and get out," he grumbled without looking away from the Playboy article he was reading. I took a half-step backwards and waited for him to spit since it sounded like he hadn't finished gargling his daily mouthful of gravel.

"You been in here half an hour," the cashier complained, finally glancing up at me. His face was an artistically engraved mask of aggravation and disappointment—in himself, me, the Easy Mart Corporation, life's rough handling of his youthful dreams, and the world's ongoing failure to make it up to him. All of it faithfully rendered in excruciating detail by the meticulous hand of fate working tirelessly against him, no doubt for decades, having started around the time his yellowed dress-shirt had last been dry-cleaned, circa 1974.

The man's eyes narrowed with suspicion. "You ain't him," he accused me spitefully. "Buck forty-nine."

I offered up a buck fifty and a magnanimous keep-the-change smile.

"What a nice surprise," came a reedy whisper from behind me.

"Him's the one," hissed the cashier, his tone a curious mix of victory and resignation.

Martin emerged from behind a rack of faded "I Love Vancouver" t-shirts. "Buy me a coffee?" He gestured vaguely with a stained paper cup and smiled wanly at the cashier.

"I'll get his coffee."

"Buck forty-nine," the man grumbled.

Martin had already ghosted out the door with the cup of joe. I spilled another buck fifty onto the counter and went after him without waiting for my change, even though I knew that the man behind the counter wasn't interested in my two cents or anybody else's.

I found Martin browsing through the parking tickets on the Hyundai.

"Any more trouble with them?" I nodded toward the car.

He looked at me blankly. "What do you want, Jake?"

"The other day you said The Norwegian was coming round telling everyone he was getting flush. I was just wondering, did he say who his supplier was?" It was a long shot but trying to find out who I was supposedly making deals with sounded a lot better than telling Nina of The Norwegian's interest in her.

Martin shook his head for a while. "Why so many tickets?" he said at last. "It's, like, throwing good paper after bad, you know? If I couldn't pay the first one, how'm I gonna pay the rest? And fuckin' wheel locks? Seriously?"

"It ain't right, no doubt. But, Martin? What about The Norwegian's new stuff? Any idea who he's getting it from?"

Martin wandered out into traffic, somehow flickering through it unharmed, and was almost to the far side of Hastings Street before he answered. Hard to make out amongst the blaring horns and revving engines, but I was pretty sure he said the "Chairman."

Chapter Twenty-two

My next stop was Revolver Coffee. There was nothing like the white noise of an espresso machine the size of a baby rhinoceros pumping out top-quality caffeine to stimulate cogitation. Not to mention the caffeine itself.

Cortado in hand, I slid into one of the wooden booths and let my mind wander. With nothing better to do, my eyes soon followed. The coffee shop was packed with a lively mix of the tattooed-and-pierced sartorially monochromatic interspersed with earth-toned boots-and-plaid entrepreneurial hipsters. Both species were endemic to the quasi-gentrified borderland Revolver occupied between downtown to the west and the affordable warehouse office space, abundant drug supply, bars, and-by-the-month hotels to the east.

None of my fellow coffee lovers looked like an opium supplier who called himself the Chairman. My gaze wandered further, up the brick wall behind the coffee bar until I was squinting absently at the bare, industrial light bulbs overhead, wishing one would light up in the idea factory I used to carry around in my hats. Instead, all I felt was a dull ache. Martin had turned out to be a dead end. Or if not dead, not quite alive either.

I studied the frothy bubbles in the bottom of the cup, but they were no tea leaves. At least I had that going for me. Only two items remained on my to-do list: call Nina to warn her that The Norwegian was interested in retaining her services, and write an actual to-do list. Not having a pen handy, I reluctantly pulled out my phone.

In a last inspired gasp of procrastination, I decided to check my e-mail before dialing her number. As luck would have it, I had one. Better yet, it was from Wendy. She had replied to a message I had sent to Dante and Richard a few days earlier with Mickey Wu's address. At first, I took it as a good sign that Wendy had gone to the trouble to dig my e-mail address out of the message history. Then I opened the message.

All it contained were three letters, a punctuation mark, and a link to an article on *The Guardian* website. Not feeling particularly satisfied with 'WTF?' I clicked on the link.

It pulled up a news article on Chip Thompson. Specifically, about him getting into a slap fight with one of the Royals at the gala fundraiser he had thrown in London for his foundation to fight child obesity. It went on to explore correlations between video games and obesity with no small measure of irony, but I didn't bother to finish the article. The last video game I played was Donkey Kong and I generally found British humour a tad superior in attitude if not quality.

More troubling than the poor health of the younger generation was the fact that Chip Thompson was spotted over in England, duking it out with a Duke around the same time he was supposed to be cruising the Strait of Georgia with Dante. The article was a couple days old, so it was possible that Chip had jumped right back on his jet to go fetch his yacht to motor up here to party with Dante. But with everything else that had been going on, I wanted to be sure.

I closed the phone's browser and opened my contacts. With a swipe of my thumb, I sailed right past 'N' and didn't stop until I reached 'R'.

Richard's phone went straight to voice-mail. By noon I

had tried him three more times and was starting to get a sense of how he must have felt when Dante dropped off the grid. Which reminded me that I also had Dante's number. Which also went straight to voice-mail.

Between attempts, I followed Wendy's lead and trawled through Internet news and gossip about Chip Thompson, hoping to shed more light on the situation. By the time I had run my phone battery into the red zone, I had only managed to learn two things: (1) Chip was still carrying a torch for my missing friend, and (2) The name of his yacht: *Dante's Inferno*.

Unable to sit still any longer thanks to an electrifying combination of caffeine and worry, I resolved to donate some old-fashioned shoe leather to further investigations. I hopped in my car and headed off to do the rounds of the local marinas.

My first stop was the Coal Harbour Marina, a short hop across downtown from Revolver Coffee. My antennae went up when I arrived to find that it had been temporarily closed to the public. Even after receiving a full-strength blast of Constable Charm, the lone, misanthropic cop at the scene would only reveal that there was an incident in progress "deemed to be a threat to public safety." From a distance, he watched me closely as I rubbernecked my way along the barricade tape, fruitlessly trying to get a look at what was going on. I was just about to give up when I spotted another man in uniform jogging toward me along the pier, holding his side. There was blood on his shirt, and he looked pale and angry.

"You okay, buddy?" I called out, as the man ducked under the tape.

He ignored me and beelined toward a nearby van without breaking stride. Emblazoned on the side of it were the words "Vancouver Animal Control."

The man had his shirt rolled up and was rummaging through a first aid kit by the time I caught up with him. "You need any help?"

"What?" he said irritably, without looking up. "No."

"That looks nasty." I gestured at the jagged laceration just below his ribs.

He paused to look at it. "Doesn't exactly feel good, but I've had worse."

I nodded. "Haven't we all."

He scowled at me. "Oh, yeah? You been gored by a goat, too?"

I stopped nodding. "That happened at the marina? What the hell is going on in there?"

"Some idiot celebrity decided to throw a rave on a yacht last night. Figured it would liven things up to have some kind of *Dungeons & Dragons* theme. There are people in there dressed up as wizards and witches, that kind of thing." He shook his head in wonderment.

"And a goat?"

He nodded. "A rabid one, at that. Or maybe it's just stoned. Either way, it freaked out and started goring people." He shouted to be heard over the siren of an arriving ambulance. "That's my cue. Gotta get back in there and help my partner." He grinned. "The goat's still got the celeb trapped in the head."

"Duty calls," I agreed. "Just one more question before you go: The celebrity, is it Chip Thompson?"

"Nah, wasn't a dude." The man closed the first aid kit with a thoughtful frown. "Some actress, I think. Kind of a hippy name. Sunny something, maybe?"

"Sunshine Holly?"

He slammed the door of the van. "That's the one."

Chapter Twenty-three

After choking down a parking ticket and a food truck hot dog, I swung by Granville Island, where I found out that a lot more people own yachts than I would've guessed. None were Chip Thompson.

I struck gold at the third marina, in Richmond, just south of Vancouver. Shoehorned into its pay parking lot was Buff's shiny purple Hummer. The receipt on the dash showed a purchase time stamp of 08:45 that morning. So it appeared that Richard, at least, hadn't failed to launch. But since the pugilistic Chip Thompson was in England, I wondered whose boat Richard and Dante were on. And had Richard managed to find something sufficiently "yachty" to wear? The parking permit was good for two days so I wasn't keen on the idea of waiting there until he got back to find out.

The salty dog in the marina office ignored me when I walked in the door. The trim, middle-aged woman behind the desk, on the other hand, wasted no time in taking my measure. She put down her newspaper and removed her reading glasses to give me a proper squint. "Help you?" she asked doubtfully.

"I hope so." I smiled at her, and then down at the dog—some kind of beagle-footstool cross—which sneezed twice before starting to groom its nether regions with an agility that belied its age and body morphology. "I'm looking for a yacht."

"We don't do rentals. Brokers' business cards are on the counter here. There's also a few private sales advertised on the bulletin board over there. You'll have to contact the owners directly." She put her reading glasses back on.

"Not to buy. Or rent. I mean a boat that was moored here. Or maybe still is."

The woman slid the spectacles down her nose and studied me closely. "You wouldn't be looking to do a repo, now would you?"

"No, ma'am, nothing like that. This is a friend of a friend's yacht. He's throwing a fancy shindig on it and my friend managed to wrangle me an invitation. Problem is, I only got his message after I got off my night shift." I yawned theatrically. "I rushed down here but I think I might have missed them. He told me which marina they were at but not the name of the boat." I chuckled and shook my head. "Any chance you'd be able to tell me which yachts sailed out this morning?"

"Can't help you."

"Listen, I totally get the privacy thing but maybe you could…"

"It's not that. We just don't keep track of our clients' arrivals and departures, so I really couldn't tell you. Even if I wanted to," she added in a tone that suggested she hadn't quite bought my repo man denial. I cursed myself for having left my blue blazer in my employee locker at the Ridge Theatre back in grade ten when I got fired for hotboxing the projection room.

"In that case, is it okay if I take a look around to see if they might still be here?"

"Not unless you have a vessel moored here. Or are a registered guest of someone who does."

"Okay, thanks anyway." I started out the door but stopped halfway and turned back, trying to look thoughtful. It was a trick I'd seen Columbo use a hundred times (counting reruns) to pry loose a critical piece of information. "Just one more thing. Truth is, I'm a bit of a yachting nerd, which is why my friend worked so hard to get me the party invitation. I don't suppose you have a list of the boats that moor here?"

The woman nodded. "Of course."

"Do you think I could...?"

"Can't help you."

"Is it the privacy thing this time?"

"Yep."

Chapter Twenty-four

It was half-past dusk by the time I made it back up to Vancouver. The drive had been slow, but it seemed like greased lightning in comparison to the evening commuter traffic headed in the other direction, crawling south in search of the excessive square footage offered by suburban homesteads and big-screen televisions.

I still hadn't heard back from Richard or Dante so I decided to stop by Wendy's condo. Two heads had to be better than one in figuring out what was going on, especially if one of them was hers. Unfortunately, the gruff hello that emanated from the intercom revealed that there would actually be three.

"Hi, Barb. Is Wendy there?"

"Who is this?" Barb's voice sounded extra strident when amplified by a cheap intercom.

"Jake Constable. We almost met last night."

"I know who you are." The roar of an arriving delivery truck drowned out her next comment. I turned and gave the driver an appreciative wave while waiting for judgment to be rendered. Intercom silence and the truck's diesel fumes had just about convinced me to abandon my mission when Wendy's voice chirped out of the tinny speaker. "Come on up."

She met me at the door, looking as confused and worried as I felt. Wendy led me through the kitchen, grabbing a couple beers from the fridge on the way. Barb was in there preparing a moss-coloured smoothie. She hit the button on the blender just as I said hello.

"Barb doesn't appear to like me much," I observed when we reached the relative quiet of the dining room.

Wendy nodded as she sat down and waved me toward a chair. "Is that a problem?"

"It seems hasty. Most people wait to get to know me first."

"She knows all about you," Wendy replied distractedly before giving me a sharp look. "Are you more worried about what Barb thinks of you or what's happened to Dante and Richard? I assume you're here because you got my e-mail this morning?"

I nodded. "Impressive sleuthing."

"More like dumb luck. I was Googling Chip Thompson this morning to see if I could find any old gossip about his relationship with Dante, or photos of them together. The article about Chip being in London just happened to be the most recent news item on him." She glared at her laptop on the table in front of her, its browser still open to *The Guardian* website. "So why the hell did Dante leave Richard a message saying he was on the guy's boat?"

"Good question. One we should definitely ask Dante once we find them."

"Assuming we do."

"Well, I've started looking. After I got your e-mail, I drove around to the marinas." I sat sat back and crossed my arms, letting one hand hover around my chin. In my mind's eye, it held a black-clay pipe. I puffed thoughtfully and waited, but not for long.

Wendy leaned forward eagerly. "Did you find anything?"

I took one more puff before answering. "The Buffmobile. Parked at a marina down in Richmond."

"That's great!" Wendy jumped to her feet and headed for the kitchen. "I'll go get Barb."

I almost choked on the smoke from my imaginary pipe. "Barb? Why?"

"She's works for the Coast Guard. She can help us find the boat."

This wasn't good news, but at least this explained how she already knew all about me—I had an unfortunate history with the Coast Guard. Barb had probably seen my mugshot up on the "Most Unwanted" board back when I was bringing boatloads of weed over from Hornby Island.

• • ● ● •

Barb clicked open her pen with natural authority. "So what's the name of the vessel that Richard and Dante went out on?"

I shrugged.

She peered at me over her old-lady reading glasses. "You didn't get the name?"

"I tried, but the woman at the marina wouldn't give me any info."

"Nothing at all?" Wendy's tone was incredulous. "When they left? Where they went?"

I shook my head "But at least now we know where the boat will come back to."

Barb snorted. "*If* it comes back."

Wendy groaned and slumped back in her chair.

Barb stood up from the table and put a hand on her shoulder. "Sorry, Wen. You know I'll do everything I can to help find Dante and Richard, but we can't search every yacht out there. Let me know if Sherlock over there comes up with any real clues."

After Barb left the room, I looked over at Wendy sympathetically. "Boy, she can be a real downer."

Chapter Twenty-five

I left Wendy's place early and went straight back to my place. Worried about Richard and Dante, and bereft of my TV and the contents of my mason jar, I spent a quiet evening at home with Tom Waits on the turntable and Don Julio in my glass. Two master emcees for the dark and distorted carnival that is the human condition.

That night, my sleep was tormented by a nightmare in which The Norwegian kicked down my door wearing a white leather sailor suit. He saluted politely and then press ganged me into joining the Coast Guard with him. We sailed around English Bay on a bathtub ferry captained by Barb in search of Dante and Richard. I finally spotted them in the distance, laughing and dancing on the deck of an immense yacht called the *Near Future*. I waved and shouted but my voice was drowned out by a dull thumping sound. The Norwegian was firing a pistol into the ocean. I pleaded with him to stop, or at least use a silencer, but he ignored me. The sea drained away through the bullet holes in the ocean floor, leaving us stranded in the tiny boat. The Norwegian gave a satisfied nod and announced that we would build the condos there.

The dull thumping sound continued after The Norwegian stopped shooting, pulling me out of the nightmare and back into my bedroom. I pulled the covers over my head and waited for the knocking to stop. Its dull, metronomic quality suggested a bleak fatalism afflicting the mind that controlled the knuckles. I could relate.

As Fate would have it, the knuckles eventually gave up. The next thing I heard perked me up quite a bit: Nina's voice calling out my name in her slightly manic, morning-person way.

It was barely eight a.m. Even if she was still just looking for a shoulder to cry on, Nina knew me well enough to realize that dropping by this early in the morning would guarantee I was still in bed. My mood improved rapidly as I considered the implications. Or at least the possibilities.

My first inclination was to wait for her right where I was, since things might lead back here quickly enough anyway. But I couldn't figure out a way to lounge in bed without feeling like a cliché. Lying on my side propped up on one elbow? Too "come hither." On my back with hands behind my head? Too "Bangkok massage parlour." Pretend to be asleep? Too "hokey porn flick." All mood killers.

Nina called my name again, now sounding slightly impatient. I made a snap decision to go with the natural approach. I jumped up and headed for the living room in what I had worn to bed—nothing. She had seen it all before and there was no need for any contrived preamble with us. The sex had always been great, even after Nina started losing interest in the rest of the marriage.

I put on an innocent, slightly sleepy smile as I walked down the hallway. It seemed a minor and forgivable affectation. "Sorry to keep you waiting. I'm just getting up, if you know what I…"

"Hello, Jake," she murmured. The look of surprise, followed by amusement, flashed across her attractive features almost too quickly to register before she locked them down into an expression of total composure.

"I don't believe you've met my uncle, Li Wei." Nina gestured to the gnome standing next her. His unfathomable age was contradicted, if not refuted, by a lustrous dome of jet black hair and ramrod posture, possibly assisted by the load-bearing suit he was wearing overtop a white dress shirt fabricated entirely from starch and buttoned tight enough to constrict my breathing. The lone splash of colour provided by his crimson tie flashed "Red Alert" more than "Life of the Party."

Standing beside him was a younger gentleman, smiling politely and wearing an identical black suit. A lover of fish, as I recalled from the first time he let himself into my apartment. His partner, the Eames fan, was not in evidence.

"Why don't I make some coffee while you get dressed?" Nina suggested smoothly.

Her prompt thawed my brainfreeze sufficiently for me to activate the motor skills required for a wordless retreat into my bedroom.

Chapter Twenty-six

I threw on a pair of boardshorts and a t-shirt with a tuxedo design on it since I didn't own anything along the lines of the funereal garb favoured by my guests. Even Nina had donned a similar outfit, though the black of her suit had a lustrous sheen and was tailored with a slightly more feminine cut.

More ominous than the uncharacteristically formal attire was her choice of shoes. I had reflexively registered them, in spite of the socially adverse circumstances. Cheap, heavy clompers with fat black laces that looked like they had come from a factory, or possibly even a factory worker, in Stalinist Russia. The only thing that stopped me from climbing out the bedroom window was the smell of fresh brewed coffee now wafting through the apartment.

It wasn't until I reached the kitchen that I remembered that Nina was a tea drinker. She had successfully employed one of my kitchen appliances to reduce coffee beans to heterogeneous rubble and divert water through it, but that's where the similarity to real coffee ended.

I gulped it down regardless. In lieu of a thank you, I remained polite when I inquired how they got in. Nina confessed she had kept a key, which, under almost any other circumstances, would have made me happy.

We returned to the living room. Rather than sitting down,

Nina assumed her previous position standing beside her uncle. As near as I could tell, neither of the men had moved an inch during our absence. Since it remained unoccupied for once, I dropped into my Eames chair. This wasn't my show but I still felt entitled to the best seat in the house. I settled in and waited for someone to say something.

Li Wei stood mute and immobile, despite the obvious deference shown to him by Nina and the younger man, who cleared his throat a couple times but otherwise remained silent. Nina frowned at her shoes distractedly.

I sighed and closed my eyes, struggling in vain to remain patient. My enthusiasm for Nina's visit had been obliterated by the company she was keeping, not to mention my resulting humiliation. And most important of all, Richard and Dante were still missing. I still didn't know how I was going to find them, but one thing was for sure; sitting there listening to Nina and her uncle breathing in stereo wasn't doing it.

I was just about to tell them as much when Nina finally started talking. It might have just been that she was speaking Mandarin but her tone sounded odd to me. I detected none of her usual self-confidence. When I opened my eyes, I found Li Wei's aimed in my direction. He gave a sharp nod when Nina finished speaking.

"My uncle would like to hire you."

"This is why you barged in on me? To arrange a house-sitting gig? I thought you told him what happened at Mickey Wu's."

"I did. That's what this is about. My uncle had a background check done on Mickey Wu and found out that he's a criminal."

I stifled a laugh, wondering whether naming tacky underwear after the leader of the Cultural Revolution qualified as a crime. "What did he do?"

Li Wei growled a few words to Nina, who nodded deferentially. "He is guilty of economic corruption," she said.

I spread my hands invitingly. "Which means what, exactly?"

"Mr. Wu is known to have transferred undeclared income out of China," said the fish lover. Li Wei looked annoyed but remained silent.

"So he's...what, a tax cheat?" I punctuated the question with a yawn.

Though his polite smile remained in place, the man's tone chilled noticeably. "It is a very serious problem in China, Mr. Constable. A number of citizens have fled our country with substantial wealth accumulated through improper means. Our Ministry of Public Security is working to locate and repatriate them so that they may make appropriate reparations for their crimes."

This more lengthy speech earned the fish lover a sharp rebuke from Li Wei, but I nodded and smiled. "Operation Fox Hunt, right? So you guys are secret agents. Very cool." The only part that didn't make sense was why Nina wasn't more relaxed, now that it was manifestly evident that her uncle was the hunter rather than the prey in whatever government investigation was under way.

I noticed that the fish lover also looked slightly uncomfortable, though I wasn't sure if this was because of my comment or the fact that Nina's uncle was plainly furious with him. Li Wei's expression hadn't actually changed a great deal but all sorts of muscles were twitching in his face, which was now approaching the colour of his tie.

Nina was looking at me with an expression of mild surprise, possibly because she had never known me to discuss, or be aware of, current events. This distraction might have been why she missed the kinetic warning signs rippling across her uncle's visage.

"Agent Wang is from the Ministry of Public Security," she explained with a nod toward the fish lover. "My uncle is the Deputy Director of the Department of Infrastructure

Development in the All-China Federation of Industry and Commerce. He came all the way from Beijing to join the investigation. His department is also involved in the corruption initiative."

"*Anti*-corruption initiative," Li Wei hissed at her in perfect English.

"Yes, of course," Nina replied as she joined the red-faced club. "It is very important for my uncle to bring these fugitives to justice," she added, her voice now little more than a whisper.

"Sounds like a job for the cops. Are you going to have Mickey Wu arrested?"

"Regrettably, China and Canada do not currently have an extradition treaty," Agent Wang said, seemingly speaking to the neon tetras.

"Meaning?" I asked, also speaking to the aquarium. I noticed that the fish had swarmed against the glass, as if monitoring our exchange intently, either in a futile attempt to make sense of the affairs of mankind, or with the slightly more realistic hope that Agent Wang would feed them.

"We are not able to compel the local authorities to arrest Mr. Wu or operate in any... official capacity."

"Sounds inconvenient. But I really don't see how I can help." I looked at Nina. "You did make it clear to them that I'm just a house-sitter now?"

She nodded, started to say something but stopped. Nina's uncle barked something at her in Mandarin. "Which means you have the alarm and keycodes for Mickey Wu's house," she said at last.

"Yeah, so?" I didn't like where this was going.

"All my uncle asks is that you get the agents inside and they'll do the rest. They just need to have a look around, check his files, that kind of thing." As she spoke, Nina waved her hands around like she was talking about doing some light dusting.

"All your uncle asks?" I looked at Li Wei, figuring I might as well try to get it straight from the horse's ass. "You're talking about breaking and entering. I don't know about China but in Canada that would be a criminal act. Committed by me."

The response came from Nina, rather than Li Wei. But she mumbled it so quickly that I had to ask her to repeat it.

The second time around, it was only slightly more audible. "I said is that a problem? You already did it once for your party."

"That doesn't mean I want to do it for your uncle's party. And, anyway, that was hardly the same thing. I was authorized to be in his house that time. I just shouldn't have brought so many friends along. More importantly, I've learned from my mistakes. There's no way I'm going back there. Especially now that Mickey Wu is home."

"He isn't," said Agent Wang

I looked over at him. "Isn't what?"

"Isn't home. My partner, Agent Chung, is watching Mickey Wu's residence as we speak. He left more than twenty-four hours ago and hasn't returned since. So there is no risk involved if we do this immediately."

"For you, maybe. But I'm already on seriously thin ice with Mickey Wu. We have a bit of an unfortunate history." I resisted the temptation to provide a detailed description of the party, though I did wonder what he would make of the albino on the scooter. Or the dead guy in the bathroom, for that matter. If he really had been the nephew of Mickey Wu's business associate, it occurred to me that the dead guy might have been another rich expat on their list. If so, the Ministry of Public Security sure wouldn't be getting any reparations from him now. I hoped Agent Wang didn't work on commission.

Agent Wang cranked up the dial on his smile. "Mr. Constable, you would be doing the government of China a great service if you assist us in bringing this criminal to justice. You have my personal assurance that your participation in our operation would be held in total confidence."

I appreciated covert ops as much as the next guy but they didn't seem like a strong foundation for a working relationship based on transparency and trust. Plus, I really didn't like Nina's uncle. "I applaud China's attempts to crack down on its tax cheats, but I've got my own criminals to bring to justice at the moment."

Bemusement turned out to be a surprisingly alluring look on Nina. "What are you talking about, Jake?"

I decided to tell her, reasoning that it might be the fastest way to get her to convince Uncle Wei and his henchmen to leave me alone. "Richard and Dante are missing."

Nina had the decency to look genuinely shocked. "What do you mean they're missing?"

"Gone. Disappeared. Under suspicious circumstances. I really don't have time to get into it right now, so if you'll excuse me…" I got up from the chair but no one else moved.

After glancing back and forth between me and her uncle, Nina looked like a deer caught in barbed wire. "I'm truly sorry to hear that, Jake. But right now, I need you to help my uncle. There's really no alternative."

Out of the corner of my eye, I saw that Li Wei was smiling like a man who just won a tug-of-war without even breaking a sweat. I ignored him and focused on Nina, unable to believe what she had just said. Or even fully understand it. "What do you mean there's no alternative?"

"I mean, if you don't help us, I will have to call the cops and tell them what you told me about having a party at Mickey Wu's house. And everything that happened at it."

"Why the hell would you do that?" I demanded.

She stared at her factory worker shoes and said nothing.

"Nina? Why would you do that to me?" I was almost shouting now. No one was smiling anymore, but I didn't care.

"I can't risk losing my business over this, Jake." Her voice grew ever quieter as mine became louder.

I took a couple breaths to calm myself before continuing. "You won't. I was the one who screwed up, so I'm the only one whose business is in jeopardy. But I've already talked to Mickey Wu and he wants to keep this thing quiet as much as I do. So this whole thing is going to go away quietly and no one's going to lose anything." Aside from the guy on the bathroom floor, of course.

Nina didn't respond, but her uncle jumped in with what sounded like some kind of rapid-fire imperative. Without looking at him, Nina nodded almost imperceptibly. "This is very important to my uncle. To our whole family," she whispered.

It finally dawned on me that it might be Li Wei who was the threat to Nina's livelihood, not Mickey Wu. Back when we were together, she had frequently boasted about how well connected he was, and how many big money clients he had sent her way. Maybe he was threatening to turn the tap off. "Nina, is your uncle forcing you to do this?" I ignored his glare.

"I need to protect myself and my family. That's all." Nina shook her head quickly. "You wouldn't understand."

I couldn't argue with that. While I stood there fuming, Li Wei issued one more set of orders in Mandarin and headed out the door with Agent Wang sailing along in his wake.

Nina's mouth was moving as she fell into step behind them but I knew that all but the last three words were her uncle's. "You are to meet Agent Wang at Mickey Wu's house tonight at eleven p.m. If you don't show up, we will call the police. I'm sorry, Jake."

Chapter Twenty-seven

After they left, I headed to Revolver in search of an antidote for the bitter taste Nina's coffee and conversation had left in my mouth. The emotional taps started to run dry about halfway through our marriage, but her betrayal still took me by surprise. Almost as much as Nina letting anyone—even her gargoyle of an uncle—tell her what to do.

With all the booths occupied, I was forced to take a seat at the long, communal table where the entrepreneurial hipster contingent of Revolver's clientele held court. I set my phone on the table in front of me and typed in a few words. While Google scoured the Internet for information on Li Wei, I eavesdropped on a man with elaborately coiffed facial hair extol the virtues of his dried seaweed food truck idea to a dreadlocked blonde. I had lost my appetite by the time the search results came back.

Li Wei's name popped up in numerous Chinese government propaganda pieces, as well as a few news articles. Judging by the evolving quality and cut of his suits in the accompanying photos, the man's climb up through the Party ranks had been a long one, during which time his hairstyle had changed very little. He had briefly served as an alternate member on the Seventeenth Central Committee but was removed when he became one of the primary targets of an official Party probe.

Into economic corruption, of all things. Most search results led to pages in Mandarin, but I did come across an English post on a defunct blog that ranted at length, and rather colourfully, about the fact that Li Wei somehow escaped conviction.

For a while after the investigation he received no media attention at all. Then his name gradually began to pop up again, predominantly as an outspoken proponent of anti-corruption initiatives, but also announcing his prestigious appointment to the All-China Federation of Industry and Commerce. I noticed that other members of that Federation had become members of the Central Committee, so it looked like Li Wei had managed to get back on track for Committee membership, despite his brush with scandal. Nina's uncle had to be more formidable than he looked if he was able to battle his way up through the ranks of the Chinese Communist Party not just once, but twice.

I was almost starting to feel guilty about the situation Mickey Wu was in. According to Nina, Li Wei hadn't even heard of him before my party, but now he had Mickey in his crosshairs. And for what? The heinous crime of underreporting China's appetite for thongs? Judging from the size of Mickey Wu's mansion, the truth about that might have caused its own scandal.

I, myself, was no stranger to undeclared income, or trying to make a fresh start. Now that The Norwegian had reappeared in my life, I was becoming painfully aware of what it was like to have past transgressions come back to haunt you. The fact was, I could relate to Mickey Wu's plight more than I cared to admit.

I might have even been tempted to warn Mickey that the guys from the Ministry of Public Security were about to break into his house, if they hadn't been forcing me to go with them. Then it occurred to me that warning him might actually solve both our problems.

If I told Mickey what Agent Wang had planned, he could simply make sure to return home before this evening. Agent Wang had already admitted that they had no official powers to investigate or arrest Mickey Wu. So if he was home, Agent Wang would simply have to abort the operation. And if he couldn't sneak in anyway, there was no need to punish me for not helping them do it.

If Nina needed any extra convincing on the last point, I could threaten to tell the press that Chinese secret agents were sneaking around trying to break into fancy Vancouver homes. Although it felt uncomfortably rat-like, I decided to let myself off on a technicality—it wouldn't get them arrested, but it would make things plenty inconvenient for them. I was no expert on covert ops, but I was pretty sure that publicity didn't help.

And speaking of not getting arrested, since Agent Wang couldn't slap the cuffs on Mickey Wu, it didn't seem like the Ministry of Public Security had much leverage to coerce or dislodge him from his new life in Canada. Which meant that if Mickey Wu knew they were coming at him, he shouldn't have too much trouble fending them off. All in all, giving him the heads-up seemed like a pretty big favour, and a good way to square things between us.

Having convinced myself that it was the right thing to do, or the least wrong thing under the circumstances, I was reaching for my phone when the first chords of "Stayin' Alive" rang out. I always get a little shiver when that happens. This time, the shiver turned into a momentary bout of paralysis when I saw the call display. Barry Gibb's electrifying falsetto was already crowing about being a woman's man by the time I cut him off and took the call.

"Hello, Mr. Wu. What a coincidence, I was just going to call you. I've been talking to some people about you recently, and I think you're going to want to know what they were saying."

"This really is a coincidence, Mr. Constable. I was about to say the exact same thing to you."

This stopped me short. "Oh?"

"Mmm-hmm. I've been entertaining some friends of yours on my yacht. They claim you actually do have the cell phone I'm looking for. Is this true, or do I need to have Thaddeus reprimand them for telling me tales?"

Knowing that only Richard and Dante could have told him this, my heart dropped all the way into my gut. The pain was visceral as the stomach acid began to eat away at it. "It's true," I admitted.

"I thought as much." I could almost hear his smirk and it sounded like it was in need of a solid punch. "After some initial resistance to answering my questions, they remained quite committed to this assertion."

"If you've hurt them—" I said angrily. Mickey Wu cut me off before I had time to come up with some appropriate threats.

"Calm down, Mr. Constable. Your friends are a bit worse for wear at the moment, but they'll be fine. Assuming you cooperate, that is. I'm prepared to view your previous denial as a misunderstanding, Mr. Constable, but I am going to have to insist that you bring me that phone without delay."

"Let me talk to Richard and Dante."

There was silence on the line, but I didn't let it last. "There's no way you're getting that phone until I know they're okay."

Mickey Wu sighed. "Please hold the line." His delivery was so blandly polite that I half expected a top-forty Muzak remix to start playing while he put me on hold. Instead, I heard a terse, muffled exchange in the background, followed by much sweeter music altogether.

"Jake?" Richard said breathlessly.

"Richard! Are you okay?"

His hesitation said much more than his words. "It's no day at the spa. But, yeah, we're okay. Thaddeus hits like a girl."

I grinned in spite of myself. "Well, if anyone would know…"

"Whatever, Constable. I kicked your ass when we were on the high school wrestling team."

"Groped it, more like. Listen, I'm coming to get you guys…."

"That's wonderful news," said Mickey Wu, having reclaimed the phone from Richard without warning. "Now that you have confirmation that your friends are okay, I trust you will do as I ask and bring me the phone?"

"If I do, will you let us all go?"

"Of course. I think you and your friends have already enjoyed more than enough of my hospitality, don't you?"

I didn't trust Mickey Wu any more than I suspected he trusted me, but doing what he asked seemed like the only shot I had to get Richard and Dante back. "I'll bring it. Where are you? What's the name of the yacht I'm looking for?"

Mickey Wu chuckled. "Just bring the phone to the Granville Island Marina at nine o'clock this evening. Oh, and I hate to sound clichéd, but come alone if you want to see your friends again."

Chapter Twenty-eight

I went home to put my affairs in order. Which is to say, I did a load of laundry and fed the fish. If I didn't make it back by morning, the tetras were just going to have to learn to take care of themselves. I was going to be tied up feeding other fish.

After that, I had a nap. It was pitch-dark when I woke up, causing me a short-lived moment of panic that I had overslept and missed the meet. My phone assured me that it was just before seven p.m. My stomach concurred.

An idea struck me. It was last-minute and low-percentage, but I knew I had to try. It could make the difference for the long night ahead. Before I had second thoughts, I was out the door and into my car.

Traffic was inexplicably light that time of day in this kind of city, so I made excellent time as I tore through the rain-soaked city streets. Much to my amazement, there was even a parking spot right out front with twenty-two minutes left on the meter. I couldn't help but think that maybe, just maybe, for once, the Fates were laughing near me, not at me.

A pair of bikers gave me the crook eye when I burst through the door. I ignored them and zeroed in on the bearded man in the red-stained smock. Before I could get to him, a twitchy reprobate with elaborately inked sleeves covering pincushion arms cut into line in front of me. I resisted the urge to slug him.

This night would be a long one, and quite possibly violent. I had to save my strength. The only thing that mattered right now was that the man in the smock wasn't turning people away. Yet.

When the reprobate had finished transacting his business with the bearded man, I stepped forward, feeling confident. But I had to know for sure. "You still got the dough?"

He wiped sweat from his brow and glanced casually at the brace of knives lying in easy reach. "I wouldn't be talking to you if I didn't."

I nodded, satisfied. "Finocchiona."

He gave me an appraising look. "Good choice."

I had barely sat down when a tired-looking woman with a safety-pin collection in each ear turned to the bearded man and drew her finger across her throat.

"That's it," he shouted. "We're out of dough for the night!" Exclamations of despair rippled through the crowd still pushing its way through the door. Those of us who had made it in time tried not to smirk as we sat at our tables.

It took the man with the beard just over four more minutes to get me the goods. I took much longer eating them, savouring each bite of fennel sausage and rapini, knowing this could turn out to be my Last Supper. If so, I couldn't have picked a better spot. Every meal at Pizzeria Farina was a religious experience.

Wiping the last traces of tomato sauce from my lips, I saw from the clock on the wall that it was time to mobilize. I headed out the door to my car. The meter ran out while my key was still in the door lock.

Before putting the car into gear, I took out my phone and sent a text to Wendy. I pulled into traffic, then immediately pulled out again and sent the same text to Nina.

> **richard and dante are on mickey wu's yacht. am going to get them back. don't call the cops.**

Chapter Twenty-nine

Tearing across town on my way to Granville Island, I made demands on my little car that the Porsche engineers probably never imagined, and certainly wouldn't condone. It was close but I made it, pulling into the parking lot at 8:58 p.m. The food markets were just closing, the tourists spilling out. I followed a family loaded down with dreamcatchers and freeze-dried salmon back to their Dodge Durango to grab their parking spot.

After that, I waited at the entrance to the marina, scanning the crowds for any sign of Mickey Wu. At 9:08 p.m., Thaddeus appeared at my shoulder. I had to hand it to him, he moved well for a squat man. Must be the tracksuit.

"Come with me," he ordered, spraying the remnants of a mouthful of candied salmon onto my canvas jacket.

I expected him to lead me into the marina where the larger boats were moored but we passed it by and continued along to the small public dock where a handful of runabouts were tied up. Apparently, we were headed out to sea. I regretted not stopping by Richard's to get something yachty to wear.

Thaddeus jumped down into a Zodiac boat tied up at the far end of the dock, landing as solidly as a portly panther. When I started to climb in after him, he put his arm out to stop me. "Hold on, Constable. You got the phone?"

I pulled it out my pocket to show him.

Thaddeus' eyes narrowed. "Finally."

"Been looking for this for a while?" I hoped to mine some information to add to my sparse supply.

He showed me a grin like rusty saw blade. "Here and there."

Even though it was arguably now a case of too little, too late, I sensed an opportunity to solve a recent crime spree. "Would that happen to include my home?"

He snorted gustily. "You call that dump a home?"

"It has a certain industrial aesthetic that's not for everyone," I admitted.

"More like a shitbox aesthetic, you ask me. Didn't anyone ever explain to you that brick is for factories? And what was with that fucking Sanyo?"

Unable to mount a defence, I decided to go the conciliatory route, show there were no hard feelings. "I've been thinking of switching to a projector."

"Smart move. The stereo, now that was alright."

"I appreciate you not messing with that."

He shrugged. "I got respect."

"You're a professional."

"Exactly."

"You did Richard and Dante's places, too?" I tried to look impressed.

"Of course. Like you said, I'm a professional."

"How'd you find them?" I figured there was no harm in asking, since it was something that actually had been bugging me.

The saw blade reappeared. "Followed you around. Led me right to 'em."

Right there, laid bare, was the difference between the professional and the amateur enthusiast. I nodded, chagrined. "There's one thing I still don't get. Why did you kidnap Dante?"

Thaddeus looked annoyed. "Yeah, that wasn't supposed to happen. I thought I heard your fruity pals leave together, but when I went into the place, he was still there." He nodded appreciatively. "The little guy put up a pretty good fight."

"So just to be clear, you've had him the whole time, right? He never was on Chip Thompson's boat?"

Thaddeus frowned. "Who the hell is Chip Thompson?"

I spread my hands. "Exactly."

"I don't know what you're talking about," Thaddeus complained.

"Don't worry about it." Thaddeus was clearly nothing more than the muscle actuated by Mickey Wu's brain. An effective combo, judging by the way they had forced Dante to lure Richard in. And me after that.

"Enough chit chat. Give it here." Thaddeus held out his hand.

"What?"

He rolled his eyes. "The phone, what else?"

I smiled at him. "Yeah, right. And then you take off and leave me here on the dock? Not a chance. I'll give it to Mickey Wu. No one else." I held the phone out over the water. "Or I could just toss it in the drink right now."

"Suit yourself." Thaddeus made a snuffling sound. It took me a minute to identify it as laughter. He waved me aboard. "Don't worry, Constable. Leaving you behind was never the plan," he said as he pushed us away from the dock and fired up the motor. I could make out more snuffling over the twin howls of the wind and the outboard as we left False Creek and headed out towards open water.

We ran without lights, at first hugging the coastline to the north, only a phone's throw from Sunset Beach Park. The myriad lights of downtown backlit athletically dressed "urban hikers" taking in the evening air. Once we cleared the beaches, Thaddeus veered west and began threading between the battered freighters anchored further out in English Bay. The brightly lit homes of Kitsilano and Point Grey to the south, and West Vancouver to the north beckoned from the receding coastline, but Thaddeus continued out into the Strait of Georgia. Maybe it was the darkness, or possibly my nerves, but the trip had a disorienting, timeless quality to it. I couldn't have said whether it took fifteen minutes or fifty.

Once we cleared the freighters, Thaddeus throttled back on the small outboard until we were nosing through the inky black water at little more than a walking pace. Seemingly out of nowhere, a yacht loomed above the water in front of us, ghostly white in the moonlight. The running lights were off but dim yellow outlines shone out around the blinds drawn over its cabin windows. Just enough light to be seen from a short distance if you knew where to look.

Thaddeus angled us in towards the stern, bringing the Zodiac close enough alongside for me to make out the name of the yacht displayed in large black script along its side: *The Chairman.*

I was still trying to guesstimate the probability that Mickey Wu's yacht had the same name as a prominent local opium supplier when Thaddeus dropped the outboard to an idle, letting us drift up to the stern of the yacht. Standing onboard was a hulking figure, his expression unreadable in the dark.

"Take that rope," Thaddeus grunted behind me. "Throw it across to him."

I gathered up the line and tossed it over. The Norwegian grabbed it without a word. He wasn't wearing a white leather sailor suit, but his presence still added a nightmarish quality to the evening's festivities. By way of a greeting, he reached across and yanked me aboard.

Chapter Thirty

Mickey Wu was waiting inside the cabin. Unlike The Norwegian, he looked every inch the yachtsman as he lounged comfortably in a captain's chair, dressed in a blue blazer with gold piping, tan slacks, and a white captain's hat.

"I used to have a blazer just like that." I surveyed the spacious cabin. It was well appointed with an abundance of teak panelling, a fully stocked wet bar, and an L-shaped leather sectional. Which was empty.

"Where are Richard and Dante?" The mere fact that I had to ask didn't bode well for any of us.

Mickey Wu smiled, waving me towards the sofa. "Would you care for a drink, Mr. Constable?"

"Sure, why not?" Something told me I was going to need a stiff one before we were done. I eyeballed his impressive selection of bourbons. "Woodford Reserve over ice. Large glass." I almost sighed out loud as I sank into the sofa's cushions. It was even more comfortable than it looked.

He waited until Thaddeus brought over my drink before speaking again. "I trust you have the phone?"

I took it out and placed it on the coffee table. "So you're into flip-phones?"

Mickey Wu hesitated. "I'm sorry?"

"Don't be. I love them, too. I assume you're a collector?

Because I can't think of any other reason you're so keen to get your hands on a phone that has nothing on it."

Mickey Wu shot me a look of alarm and snatched the phone off the table. After his thumbs danced around the buttons for a few seconds, he froze, his tense poker face slowly melting into a small, soft smile.

"Oh, right, I almost forgot about the photos." From his expression, it seemed a safe bet that he was looking at the picture of the girl rather than the bank. "She sure is a hotty." I hoped a play to his ego would get him boasting and elicit some information about her.

Mickey Wu's smile was gone in an instant. His eyes narrowed along with his vocal chords as he hissed, "You are talking about my daughter."

"Your...you must be very proud," I mumbled, mentally giving myself a pat on the back for uncovering information that did indeed throw things into a new light. One that temporarily blinded me.

Mickey Wu flared his nostrils rather dramatically before returning his attention to the phone. He mooned over his daughter a bit more before pulling up the photo of the bank. After contemplating it for a moment, Mickey snapped the phone shut with an air of finality I couldn't help but find disconcerting. Rather than speculate on his intentions, I tried to make sense of this new information.

When The Norwegian told me that his run-in with the dead guy had been about blackmail, I assumed that he was the one shaking down the dead guy on behalf of his Mystery Boss. Now that I knew the guy in the bathroom had been carrying around a photo of Mickey Wu's daughter, it seemed more likely that Mickey Wu was the one being blackmailed.

Which meant that Mickey's story about the dead guy being the cousin of one of his business associates was a load of crap. No real surprise there. I tried my best to believe it because it made my problems with Mickey Wu go away, and finding out that the Chinese Ministry of Public Security was after Mickey Wu had helped—if he was one of the targets for Operation Fox Hunt, it seemed plausible that the people he did business with might be as well. Especially since Agents Wang and Chung were flashing the dead guy's mugshot around.

The fact that the dead guy had somehow dug up compromising information on Mickey Wu's daughter in order to blackmail him suggested he was more hunter than fox. But if the dead guy wasn't another corrupt business man being targeted by Operation Fox Hunt, why would the Ministry be looking for him? I found myself wishing that I could head back to the public library to ask Mr. Two Hats if he could provide me with the solution to another puzzle.

And then he did. "You're not the only one who can figure out the tough clues," I muttered aloud. "Or wear two hats."

"What did you say?" Mickey Wu asked, with understandable confusion.

I gave him a knowing smile, taking time to let the moment ripen. "The man on your bathroom floor was blackmailing you, correct?"

For a split second Mickey Wu looked surprised, then his face rapidly reconfigured into a grimmer version of my smile. He nodded. "'Was' being the operative term."

I saw his nod and raised a finger of accusation. "He also worked for the Chinese Ministry of Public Security, didn't he?"

This time, Mickey Wu didn't even attempt to conceal his surprise. "How could you know that?"

"A couple of his colleagues paid me a visit the other day." I said with a shrug. "I put two and two together." There didn't seem to be any need to mention that I only finished the math a few seconds ago.

The fact that the dead guy was an agent explained why the Ministry was wondering where he had disappeared to. During his covert investigation of Mickey Wu, he had evidently dug up information on Mickey's daughter. Something the Ministry could use to force Mickey to return to China—or at least make a generous, tax-deductible contribution to the Communist Party. But instead of reporting it, the agent went rogue and tried to blackmail Mickey Wu. Which explained why the Ministry was trying to track him down.

As I worked through the angles in my head, I noticed that Mickey Wu was watching me intently. Something approaching panic was not quite hidden in his gaze. "What did you tell them?"

I took a sip of bourbon. Then I took another, buying myself time to consider how to proceed. Mickey Wu watched me while he played nervously with the phone he had been so desperate to get his hands on. It gave me an idea. "What did I tell them, Mr. Wu? Or what did I show them?"

His eyes flicked reflexively downwards.

I smiled conspiratorially. "Don't worry, I didn't show them that photo of your daughter."

Mickey Wu didn't say anything, but the way he visibly relaxed spoke volumes.

"What don't they know about her?" I asked, hoping to capitalize on whatever modicum of goodwill I had managed to generate by inadvertently keeping his confidence.

For a moment I didn't think he was even going to answer my question. "That she exists," he said at last.

I nodded slowly. "That's big."

"At great personal cost, I have taken precautions to keep my daughter at a distance. Hidden, so that she cannot be used against me." Mickey Wu sighed. "But she is impetuous, and came to visit me, despite my orders to the contrary. It was meant to be a happy surprise." He shook his head sadly. "She has no idea what is at stake."

I nodded slowly, recalling the accounts of the family members of Operation Fox Hunt targets being harassed, allegedly even kidnapped, by the Chinese government. I was on the verge of feeling sympathetic until I remembered the dead agent on the bathroom floor.

I wondered what Li Wei would say when he found out that a member of the Party had attempted such a sordid form of economic corruption as blackmail. No doubt he would be Officially Outraged, and also possibly annoyed that he hadn't thought of it first. Sure, the Ministry guys were issued stylish black suits and red ties, but it was hard not to envy Mickey Wu's swanky lifestyle. I could see how someone with a crappy job and frayed moral fibre might stoop to questionable means to help himself to a piece of what Mickey had.

Which now included the blackmailer's phone. So I stopped worrying about threats to the integrity of the Chinese Communist Party and started worrying about saving three asses that meant a lot more to me: Richard's, Dante's, and my own. "I'm happy to have helped you clean up some loose ends. Getting back to Richard and Dante…"

Mickey Wu offered me the thinnest of smiles. "I am grateful that you have returned the phone. And that you didn't show the photo of my daughter to the men from the Ministry, Mr. Constable. Now, if you'll excuse me."

Belatedly, I realized that I had purchased some mildly interesting information at the cost of my leverage with Mickey Wu. Now that he knew I hadn't shown Agents Wang and Chung the photo, my status had switched from potential threat to another loose end.

Chapter Thirty-one

Thaddeus ignored my suggestion that he freshen up my drink while Mickey Wu was visiting the head. Probably for the best, since I was going to have to keep my wits about me to talk my way out of this.

I took a shot at it as soon as Mickey got back. "Getting rid of me isn't going to solve your problems. Sure, The Norwegian deep-sixed the agent who was blackmailing you, and might even be convinced to do the same to me, but that won't change the fact that the Ministry knows you're here. They're going to keep coming at you." I was grasping at straws, but if I got my hands on enough of them maybe I could build myself a life raft.

Leather creaked as The Norwegian crossed his arms. "I told you, Constable, I'm going legit. I don't do that stuff anymore. But keep it up and you might just convince me to give you a beat down."

I held up my hands in what I hoped was a calming manner. "Hey, I'm sure you were only trying to put a scare into him. I know it's not precision work."

The Norwegian's expression gave me pause, not just out of concern for personal safety. I was also somewhat taken aback by an unmistakable aura of wounded sincerity.

"You really only paid him off?" I asked.

The Norwegian nodded emphatically, now looking genuinely exasperated with me.

"Then how'd he end up dead?" We both looked over at Mickey Wu.

"The guy's dead?" The Norwegian asked.

"What of it?" Mickey Wu snapped. Apparently, he didn't like being challenged, even by Scandinavian man-mountains.

"Why didn't you tell me?" The Norwegian's voice dropped to an ominous growl. "You setting me up to take the fall for that?"

"Of course not. Your task was legitimate. You were supposed to pay the man off in exchange for the phone and the safety-deposit box key, then go and retrieve the documents on my daughter from within it. But you failed to accomplish this." Mickey Wu gave a "see what you made me do" shrug.

The Norwegian threw his hands up angrily, making the cabin suddenly seem very small. "I told you, that wasn't my fault. He was already inside the house when I arrived, scurrying around Constable's party like a frightened rabbit. When I tried to take him back outside, he got spooked and locked himself in the bathroom. Said he didn't know me so he wouldn't deal with me."

Mickey Wu nodded impatiently. "And that's why I sent Thaddeus over to deal with the matter."

Thaddeus bared his nicotine-stained canines at me. "Guy just needed to see a friendly face, is all."

"And, as of right now, we have everything tidied up," Mickey Wu continued. "So there's really nothing for you to be concerned about. Once you have helped me take care of my business tonight, I will be free to help you with yours."

The Norwegian considered this in silence.

As did I. It seemed I owed The Norwegian an apology for messing up his business, after all. He hadn't been able to impress his new boss by handling a simple payoff in exchange for a phone and a key. At least I had made it up to him by bringing the phone. But it occurred to me that Mickey Wu was wrong about all the loose ends being tied up. "I also found a key on the dead agent. Maybe it's the one you're looking for?"

Thaddeus snorted. "Nice try, goofball." He grabbed a chain around his neck and pulled it up to show a small silver key. It looked like the kind used to open safety-deposit boxes. "I took it off Mr. Secret Agent man myself right after I bounced him off the water fountain in Mr. Wu's bathroom."

"Sounds like thirsty work. I hope you helped yourself to a drink from it afterwards. But if you're so good at fetching, why didn't you take his phone, too, and save your boss all this trouble?" I asked, still hoping to sow some dissension in the ranks.

Thaddeus glared at me. "I did."

"But not the right one," Mickey Wu scolded.

"He was holding a phone so I grabbed it," Thaddeus protested. "I even checked it like you told me by calling the number he texted the picture of your daughter from, and the bloody thing rang. How was I supposed to know he had switched the SIM card into a new phone?"

Thaddeus' discomfort brought me a fleeting moment of satisfaction. It also explained why the phone I found on the dead guy had no SIM card in it. The call log on it showed that he had first made a six-minute call to Mickey Wu, followed by a much shorter one to The Norwegian. After that, the dead guy had apparently transferred the SIM card to a different phone, perhaps because he suspected he was being double-crossed when Mickey told him The Norwegian was handling the payoff. Or maybe the dead guy was planning to hand over the phone with the pictures but had a great phone number he wanted to keep, one that spelled out "spy dude" or "cash cow," and Thaddeus bashed the guy's head in before he had a chance to hand over the right one.

"You did your best," Mickey Wu assured Thaddeus in a soothing tone. "The trick with the SIM card was unanticipated."

"Almost as clever as killing the guy in your boss' house. Nice way to get him a murder rap," I interjected. I was in no rush for them to patch things up and move on to other business. Such as dealing with me.

Thaddeus doubled down on his scowl, but Mickey Wu merely smiled. "Except I was out of town, wasn't I? An upstanding businessman out for a cruise on my yacht while, unbeknownst to me, the sanctity of my home was being violated by a gang of depraved low-lifes. If the police had been summoned, we both know who they would've suspected."

We did, indeed. I glanced at one of the depraved low-lifes who had been at my party to see if he was following along. Sure enough, The Norwegian hadn't failed to grasp the risk to which Mickey Wu had exposed him. He was even looking grumpy about it.

"Great that you had a solid alibi. Particularly one that conveniently positioned you to disappear if things went wrong that night. Too bad you didn't make similar arrangements for your employees."

Thaddeus looked befuddled, as if he suspected I was referring to him but couldn't figure out why. Mickey Wu caught my meaning instantly. His eyes widened slightly as he appraised The Norwegian's simmering rage. "Unfortunately, that wouldn't have been possible. Which is why I have gone to such efforts to clean things up. The body will never be found—"

"But if it is," I cut him off, "the man was an employee of the Chinese government…"

"A covert agent," he countered, butting in on my interruption. All Mickey Wu and I needed were matching windbreakers and we could pass for an old married couple. "His identification documents were forged. Totally untraceable even if his remains were found. Which they won't be." Mickey Wu smiled at me. "No police, no body, and no witnesses—I'd say that adds up to no crime."

Judging from his expression, The Norwegian seemed to agree. And if I was honest, he pretty much had me convinced as well.

Some people had a natural sense of timing and Mickey Wu was clearly one of them. Both his carefully timed entrance after the party, and now. He smiled at The Norwegian as he rose from his chair. "Why don't you come along with me and we can discuss any lingering doubts you might have? Thaddeus will stay here to take care of Mr. Constable."

Without so much as a good-bye, Mickey Wu disappeared out the door. The Norwegian gave me an apologetic shrug and followed him.

Chapter Thirty-two

"They're not coming back, are they?"

Thaddeus merely grinned in response.

I swirled the last of the ice around in my glass. It really was a big one, just like I asked for. Heavy, too. Crystal, from the look of it. The thing probably cost as much as my aquarium. When I looked up, Thaddeus was screwing a silencer onto an automatic pistol.

It was depressing but also a bit ironic. Thaddeus was exactly the kind of knucklehead I brought The Norwegian in to deal with. "Are Richard and Dante even onboard?"

He shook his head. Still grinning.

I held up my glass. "Any chance of a last drink?"

Thaddeus raised the pistol. "Get up. We're going outside."

I looked down at the thick, beige, undoubtedly expensive carpet—not even Richard and Dante would have been able to get blood out of it. "Mickey Wu gave you a scolding about making a mess in the house, didn't he? Sorry, but I'm not feeling too motivated to help you out."

"Suit yourself." He casually lowered the angle of the pistol until it was pointed at my Joe Boxers. "But I'll make it hurt a lot more."

"Alright, alright. Have it your way." None of this was proving to be as easy as pulp fiction had led me to believe.

As I stood up, the windows began to strobe with a flashing blue light.

"Attention crew of *The Chairman*, this is the Coast Guard. Your vessel is being operated in an unsafe manner due to lack of proper running lights, as required by the Canada Shipping Act. Present yourselves above-deck immediately and prepare for boarding and inspection."

Thaddeus froze like a deer in the headlights. Or a goon in the spotlight, as a powerful beam of light swept across the deck of *The Chairman*, its glare briefly flooding the cabin around us.

When he squinted toward the window in confusion, I hurled my glass at him. With surprising speed he brought his arm up to block it, yelping in pain and dropping the pistol as the tumbler deflected off his wrist and shattered on the wall behind him. Thaddeus snarled and lunged toward me. I barely managed to kick the coffee table into his legs as he came on, sending him sprawling.

I dove onto him, hearing the air go out of him as I landed. I followed up with a fast right hook but got nothing more than his ear and rugburn as he writhed beneath me. His arms flailed with a purpose I recognized only belatedly.

Thaddeus hugged himself to me, trapping my left arm. I tried another punch with my right, but he anticipated it and torqued hard, rolling me onto my side so I couldn't swing effectively. Next thing I knew he had his legs wrapped around me as well. After that, he just lay there, pinning me and squeezing with all his strength. Which was considerable.

"This is stupid," I managed to grunt. Thaddeus' nasty grin suggested that he disagreed. I soon understood why. The seconds ticked by and dizziness began to overtake frustration as I pined for oxygen.

The sound of our laboured breathing was suddenly drowned out by another—the outboard on the Zodiac firing up. We both froze, listening as the motor revved briefly before starting to fade away.

"There goes your ride," I wheezed.

Thaddeus relaxed his grip slightly as he twisted around to look toward the stern with a befuddled look on his face. I pushed hard with my leg to try to roll him onto his back. When he braced against it, I rocked back sharply in the other direction, managing to pull my right arm free. I began to hammer my forearm into the side of his face. It was like pummeling a cinderblock. The stubble on his jaw was giving me more rugburn, but I was reasonably confident that he was getting the worst of it.

The next time I hit him, he bit my arm. My jacket saved me from needing a rabies shot but it still hurt. When I pulled my arm away, he shimmied up me like a lumberjack climbing a tree and wedged his shoulder into my throat.

I hammered weak blows onto his back as my air supply was once again cut off. An attempt to yank his hair availed me nothing more than a greasy handful of Brylcreem. I grabbed at his shirt next, but the material was just as slippery as his perm.

Finally, I got hold of the chain around his neck. It bit into my fingers as I twisted it so I knew it must be doing the same to Thaddeus' neck. And sure enough, the pressure on my throat started to ease slightly. Until the chain snapped and came away in my hand.

On the edge of blacking out, I couldn't initially comprehend why Thaddeus abruptly changed his method of attack to squealing and flopping around like a freshly caught tuna. It was undeniably bruising, but not nearly as incapacitating as his python routine. With little more than an encouraging nudge from me, he finally threw himself clear altogether.

Newly unencumbered, I managed to raise my head enough to see a pair of black leather boots. Smartly creased navy pants protruded from the top of them and continued all the way up to a blaze-orange bomber jacket. Sandwiched between that and a beret was Barb's stern face. In her hand was my

TV remote control. Or possibly Wendy's stun gun. Or maybe even her own.

"Hey, great to see you," I gasped, stuffing Thaddeus' chain, along with the safety-deposit box key, into my pocket.

Barb looked dubious.

"No, really. How'd you find me?"

"Wendy called. Said you texted to tell her that Dante and Richard were on a yacht owned by a guy named Mickey Wu." Her frown deepened as she surveyed the scene. "And that you were going out to rescue them."

I took the high road and ignored her sarcastic tone. "How did you know which boat was Mickey Wu's?"

"She told me which marina he uses. I called, identified myself, and asked for the name of his vessel. Simple," Barb said with a shrug. "We located it on AIS. That's the Automated…"

"Identification System. Yeah, I know."

"Oh, right, I forgot. You're already familiar with what we do."

Again with the sarcasm. Only recently re-oxygenated, my brain struggled to come up with a suitably cutting retort.

"So where are they?" Barb asked at last.

"I don't know about the pilot of this tub, but Mickey Wu and The Norwegian took off in a Zodiac. I take it they got away?"

"I mean Dante and Richard."

"Oh. Yeah. I don't think they're onboard." I lay back on the floor and stared up at the ceiling, feeling tired and beaten as the adrenaline drained out of me. "I don't know where they are."

The next thing Barb said made me feel even worse.

"Captain Constable, sir!"

I rotated my head painfully to witness the arrival of a second pair of boots. From there, my eye reluctantly travelled up an even sharper set of trouser creases, past more blaze-orange, and stopped just south of the owner's grey brush cut.

"Hi, Mom."

• • ● ● •

Things had been tense between us for the past few years. Ever since her patrol vessel responded to the distress call I put out when I ran aground transporting a harvest back from Hornby Island one night. I'm not sure which had been the more mortifying discovery for her—the bales of marijuana bobbing up out of the back of my granddad's boat as it sank, or the fact that I couldn't read a tidal chart properly.

She scrutinized me with a clinical eye. "Are you injured?"

"Not really, I just…"

"Good. In that case, why don't you tell me what the hell is going on?"

Where to start? The party? Mickey Wu? The Norwegian? Definitely not the dead guy. We had barely spoken since the night she found out I was a pot dealer so maybe it would help to start with a bit of context.

"Well, Mom, you'll be happy to hear I got a new job…"

Chapter Thirty-three

Moments before the VPD Marine Unit arrived to take custody of *The Chairman*, my mom ordered me to disappear below deck in a rare display of maternal protectiveness. Or maybe she had done it simply because she couldn't send me to my room. Either way, I was relieved. After hearing my heavily edited explanation of how I had come to be on Mickey Wu's yacht, my mom seemed to be seriously considering handing me over to the police. To my amazement, Barb spoke up in my defence, pointing out that I was only trying to save my friends.

As soon as the Coast Guard patrol vessel pulled away from *The Chairman*, I texted Mickey Wu:

the cops have Thaddeus. i have the safety deposit box key.

I received his response almost instantaneously, though it took me a moment to recognize the photo of the bank from the dead guy's phone. By the time I had, his second one had arrived:

The documents in exchange for your friends.

Perfect. Now all I had to do to get Richard and Dante back was break into a bank.

Chapter Thirty-four

It was past midnight by the time I was back on dry land and heading home. I was sitting in the passenger seat of Barb's Subaru Forester, watching the halo of light in the sky slowly grow brighter as we approached Vancouver at precisely the speed limit. The only thing stopping me from grabbing Barb's leg and pushing her foot down on the accelerator was the fear that she would think I was making a pass at her.

"Thanks for smoothing things over with my mom back there."

Barb continued to watch the road, both hands on the wheel, prudently placed at the ten and two positions. "I did it for her sake, not yours."

"Okay, then, thanks for tracking down *The Chairman* and bringing in the cavalry."

"I was looking for Dante and Richard, same as you."

I sighed. "Thanks for the ride?"

"Wendy made me promise to give you one."

I gave up, content to let the rest of the trip pass in silence.

"You could be nicer to your mother, you know."

A few mile markers later, Barb tried again. "Did you hear what I said?"

I nodded.

"Well?"

"Well, for one thing, it's none of your business." Screw silence. And politeness. "And for another, what the hell do you know about it, anyway?"

"I know you haven't called her in years."

"Not true. I called her last year on her birthday."

"To borrow money."

Okay, so maybe Barb knew a little about it. "But at least I called, which is more than she can say. What's that about? A mother not speaking to her son?"

"Maybe she's waiting for you to thank her. Or at least apologize."

"For what?" I asked in a tone that I hoped would pass for innocent.

Barb snorted. "Responding to your S.O.S., obviously."

Blame it on fatigue, but I couldn't help but blow a raspberry. "She was doing her job. You know how I know? Because she told me so that night."

"What she was doing was putting her career on the line to save your butt from going to jail. Just like tonight. I didn't hear you thank her for that either."

"Ah, yes, her career. Don't worry, I'm very familiar with its importance." I didn't really care that my mom had revealed that I used to drive around in boats filled with weed, but I was a bit perturbed that she would complain about it to a colleague instead of to me.

"Second only to you."

My laughter caused Barb to take her eyes off the road for the first time. When she looked at me, I couldn't hide my surprise at seeing hers.

"Don't you know how important you are to her?" she asked.

"Not really, no. Remember the part where she and I haven't spoken for years?"

"Did it ever occur to you that she might be hurt?"

"Yeaahhh, no. Again, not really."

"Well, I assure you she is. Deeply." Barb weighted the ensuing silence with disapproval.

"Mmmmm, I think you're confusing embarrassment with being hurt."

Barb snorted again and shook her head.

I studied Barb suspiciously. "She told you she was hurt?"

Barb looked uneasy. "Not in so many words. But I can tell."

I laughed again, this time with genuine relief. For a moment, she almost had me convinced that stoic, stiff-upper-lipped Captain Constable felt hurt. Or any emotion other than pride in her own career and shame in mine. Such a bizarre and unexpected turn of events could only lead to unwelcome surprises. Like feelings of my own—e.g., guilt.

"She's an amazing woman, you know. Strong, intelligent, professional. Captain Constable has been a real mentor for me."

Barb's usual tone of voice made it sound like she was reading heavily redacted wartime announcements. Come to think of it, maybe she was, when speaking to me. But her estimation of my mom's character, which I was unable to confirm or deny from firsthand experience, sounded like a schoolgirl whispering into a telephone on a Sunday morning in May, circa 1958. When I glanced over, the dreamy expression on her face provided the confirmation I needed. "Aw, crap. You've got a crush on my mom, don't you?"

Her cheeks flushed red and she made a strange sound, something between a cough and a yelp.

I sighed from deep down within. "Don't worry. I won't tell Wendy."

Neither the wartime announcer nor the schoolgirl had a reply, but Barb did manage to shoot me a look like I was crazy. I grinned back at her to show her that I knew a pathetic attempt at denial when I saw one.

When the emotional dust settled, I noticed that we were

headed for the Granville Street Bridge, presumably because it led toward her home. "My car's parked down by Granville Island, so you could drop me off anywhere along here."

"Wendy wants to see you," Barb grumbled.

I decided my car could wait.

Chapter Thirty-five

Wendy gave me a big hug as soon as we walked through the door. "I'm so glad you're okay." Before I had a chance to reciprocate, or even appreciate, her embrace, she pushed away and looked past me into the empty hallway. "Where are Dante and Richard?"

"I don't know," I admitted. "They weren't on Mickey's boat."

I gave her a rundown of the night's events and revelations. We shook our heads over the sordidness of the blackmail angle. Both she and Barb were suitably wowed by the gloss of international espionage the agents of Operation Fox Hunt brought to the whole affair. When we got to my failure to liberate Richard and Dante, the declining value of my stock was obvious from their facial expressions. I knew exactly how they felt.

The brief bump it received during my description of how I had heroically subdued Thaddeus was rudely undermined by Barb's tedious obsession with the facts of the matter. In the end, though, even she was grudgingly impressed that I had come away with the key to the safety deposit box, once I explained its significance.

"But Mickey Wu still has Dante and Richard," Wendy concluded pointedly.

"What an asshole," Barb opined.

"Sure, but remember, he is between the sword and the wall."

"Only because of his own malfeasance," Barb retorted.

"But what about the malfeasance of the Chinese government in all this?" I pointed out.

Barb harrumphed. "What has it done wrong, aside from attempting to bring criminals to justice? Which I suppose you might find unpalatable."

Wendy had begun pacing like a tiger in a modestly sized condominium. "Whose side are you on, Jake? Mickey Wu kidnapped Richard and Dante."

I held up my hands in surrender. "You're right. We have to nail this guy."

To bolster everyone's spirits, I vowed to retrieve the documents from the safety-deposit box and deliver them to Mickey Wu in exchange for the safe return of our beloved Buff boys.

Barb looked dubious but Wendy gave me a hopeful look. "Great," she said. "How?"

"Simple. Mickey Wu sent me a photo of the bank where they're being held. And the box number is conveniently engraved on the key right here." I held it out for their inspection.

"What was the dead guy's name?" Wendy asked.

I shrugged. "Who cares?" I had already sat through the Nancy Drew routine with Nina and didn't feel like wasting more time wondering about irrelevant details.

"I don't," she replied. "But the bank will."

"Why?"

"You've never had a safety deposit box, have you?" Wendy asked.

I shook my head. "Up until today I wasn't aware they still existed outside of Hollywood movie sets."

"Well then, maybe you recall from those movies that you have to sign for access to the box. And show some ID."

Setback. Not for the first time, I found myself regretting that I hadn't committed more fully to a life of crime. I'd had the chance to take the dead guy's wallet along with his phone, but like some kind of Boy Scout trying for a merit badge in Postmortem Etiquette, I had foolishly left it in Mickey Wu's bathroom.

Which meant he should still have it.

"Hold on a minute." I pulled out my phone and texted Mickey Wu. A moment later, I received a response in the form of a photo of the dead guy's driver's licence. I held up my phone to show it to Wendy and Barb, who for some reason looked less than impressed.

"Great, so now we know his name. But the bank isn't going to accept that photo as ID," Wendy said. "Plus, that dude is Chinese."

I nodded glumly. "Did I forget to mention that part?"

Chapter Thirty-six

We drank bottles of Gypsy Tears and tried to figure out what to do. When the beers were gone, we switched to tequila. Serious work required serious drinking, was the thinking, which became steadily less cogent as the night wore on.

"Why don't you trade the key for Dante and Richard? Mickey Wu has the ID, so let him impersonate the dead man," Barb suggested.

Wendy nodded. "Even if Mickey Wu doesn't want to risk impersonating the dead guy, once he has the key, he can at least be sure that no one else can get the documents to blackmail him again."

"It's tempting," I admitted. "But I don't trust the guy. Look what happened when I showed up with the phone. Rather than handing over Richard and Dante, he tried to give me to Thaddeus as a snack."

Barb hooked her thumbs in her belt like a sheriff in a Spaghetti Western. "And where's Thaddeus now?"

"That's right." Wendy's tone was mischievous as she put a comforting hand on my arm. "Your mommy didn't let the bad man hurt you."

"Hold on, Wen. Let's be fair. Jake didn't need his mom to save him." Barb reached over and gave my other arm a squeeze. "I was the one who did that."

Unable to come up with any pithy comebacks, I took the high road and ignored them. "Mickey Wu sees me as a loose end. Richard and Dante, too. If I hand over everything he wants, there's no way the three of us are walking out of there."

Wendy and Barb said nothing. I waited patiently, hoping they would come up with a way to refute my bleak assessment of our chances.

The silence stretched on until I broke it myself. "The only way this is going to work is if I get the documents and make copies of them. I'll leave those with you as an insurance policy against any lingering homicidal intentions Mickey Wu may have."

"Good thinking." Barb gave me two thumbs up. "Which brings us back to the question of how you're going to get them."

I marinated my tongue with a sip of liquid courage before telling them my idea. "I know a guy who makes fake IDs."

Wendy exchanged a look with Barb and grabbed my phone from the coffee table. "You really think the bank is going to believe your name is…" She squinted at the screen. "Zhang Tao?"

"I'm not saying it's going to be easy."

"I'd settle for something within the realm of possibility," Wendy muttered.

Barb tapped her chin thoughtfully. "Maybe Jake's onto something here."

Wendy and I looked over at her in surprise.

"I am?" I asked cautiously.

Barb nodded. "Obviously, the idea is half-baked, but that's to be expected, coming from you."

It might've been because she was the only one of us not drinking tequila, but I somehow found her derision more comforting than her support. I listened attentively.

"It could work," Barb continued. "If the fake ID really is a good one?" She gave me a searching look.

I waved it off. "The best."

Barb's look searched a little longer before she nodded. "In that case, all we need is a Chinese man."

It was nice to see Barb get a helping of Wendy's withering incredulity for a change. "Do you have one handy?" she asked.

"Well…no," Barb replied.

"Who we can convince, coerce, or manipulate into committing fraud for us?" Wendy added.

Barb's cheeks reddened. "I'm only trying help."

I was loath to derail their exchange, since it had all the signs of a tiff in the making, but Barb's rather obvious point had broadened my own view of the situation. Too long a pawn in all of this, I had failed to look at the whole board when trying to devise a strategy for getting our queens back.

"I do."

Wendy glanced over at me irritably. "You do what?"

"I have a Chinese man handy. Two, actually." Secret Agents Wang and Chung had much to recommend them, so I did. "These guys are perfect for the job. They share the same profession, tailor, and inclination to operate outside of the law as the dearly departed. If anyone can pass for him, it's one of them."

Barb smiled and extended her hand toward me, palm up, as if she was introducing the keynote speaker at a maritime law conference. "There you go."

Wendy ignored her. "Who are these guys?"

"Agents from the Chinese Ministry of Public Security. Just like the dead guy."

Barb withdrew here hand. "And you know them how?" She asked in a way that suggested she was preparing to endure the lame punchline to an ill-timed joke.

"Had 'em over for coffee the other day," I replied, nonchalantly.

Wendy grinned and shook her head. "You move in strange circles, Constable."

"Hold on a minute. Not everyone suffers from your utter lack of moral fibre." Barb's voice was taut with misplaced collegial outrage. "What makes you think you can convince government representatives to commit a criminal act?"

I shrugged. "Because they already tried to convince me to commit one."

Barb spluttered with indignation but Wendy listened attentively while I explained how Li Wei and the gang had tried to coerce me into letting them into Mickey Wu's house.

"So you could offer them a quid pro quo," she summarized when I was finished.

"Exactly. If they help us get what's in the safety deposit box, I'll help them get into Mickey Wu's house."

Wendy frowned. "But they're colleagues of the dead guy."

"Yup. But these guys want to arrest Mickey Wu, not blackmail him."

She waved away this distinction. "Aren't they going to take a keen professional interest in the contents of the safety deposit box when they find out it belonged to Zhang Tao? If he was using those documents to blackmail Mickey Wu, that must mean that the Ministry of Public Security wants them."

"Good point. It's a safe bet that they'll be disinclined to part with them once they get their hands on them. Which would put us back at square one, with no leverage and nothing to trade for Richard and Dante." I slumped back into my seat to ruminate on this.

"Maybe you can get the documents away from them before they know what they've got," Barb suggested, her mind apparently back in the game despite the evident disapproval that continued to sour her expression.

"But they'll know they've got something important as soon as they find out the documents belonged to Zhang Tao," Wendy said.

"So don't tell them. A field agent should only be given the minimum necessary information required to complete the mission at hand." Barb's shrug conveyed a casual but compelling authority. "Basic operational parameters for any chain-of-command organization."

"Whoever I get to do this is going to have to know whose name he was signing eventually, but I could probably delay telling them until we arrived at the bank." I was dismayed to find myself looking to Barb for approval.

She nodded. "If you can accomplish that, you might be able to get the documents away from them before they have a chance to look at them. If these guys are well-trained and disciplined, they will exit the operational theatre before attempting information-analysis."

"You mean they'll get the hell out of the bank before looking at the documents?" I asked.

"Affirmative."

As our eyes met, Barb and I shared a brief but unmistakable moment of mutual respect. I resisted a sudden urge to salute her by reaching for my drink instead. "That's a pretty small window of opportunity. Provided there's only one of them, and I went into the safety deposit box room with him, I suppose I might be able to grab the documents. But Agents Wang and Chung are going to want to see them at some point."

"Maybe you could swap in something else in place of the real documents," Wendy suggested.

I grinned. "This is great. I've always wanted to pull off a heist. If it works out, maybe for our next caper we can steal a priceless statuette with an ancient curse on it."

Wendy and Barb exchanged a look, which was better than an outright "no."

"The fakes would have to be something pretty compelling, if they're going to believe that their colleague was blackmailing Mickey Wu with them."

I raised a finger. "Now that you mention it, they aren't currently aware that he was blackmailing Mickey Wu. I'm pretty sure that all they know at this point is that Zhang Tao is MIA."

"Doesn't matter," said Barb. "Once you mention their colleague, all that is going to have to come out. Maybe not while you're at the bank. But you can bet they're going to want answers the minute you're out of there."

I very much wanted to disagree with Barb, if only as a matter of policy. But there was no way around the fact that she was right. "Okay, then, what can I possibly swap in to throw Agents Wang and Chung off the scent?"

Chapter Thirty-seven

"Pornography."

Barb looked over at me disapprovingly.

"What? She said it, not me," I protested, pointing at Wendy.

"Yes, but you don't have to look so happy about it," Barb retorted.

"I'm just pleased that she's offering up some ideas. All you seem to do is criticize."

"Quit sniping, both of you," Wendy cut in. "Can we please focus on my idea, since it's the only one on the table."

"Pornography," I prompted helpfully.

Barb looked over at me disapprovingly.

"Exactly. It's perfect," said Wendy.

"I totally agree."

"Oh, really? And why is that?" Barb snapped, still staring at me.

Wendy looked at me inquiringly.

"I don't want to steal your thunder," I said graciously. "Go ahead and explain it to Barb."

"It's simple, really. Can you imagine anything more awkward and embarrassing than looking at porn with your banker? Or with Jake, for that matter?"

I chose to ignore Barb's unladylike guffaw.

"So if Agent Wang does decide to take a peek at the documents," Wendy continued, "one look at a nice, glossy 8x10 beaver shot should put an end to his inquisitive inclinations in a hurry. All Jake needs is a manila envelope full of nudie pics. The more amateurish the better."

"Check his pockets." Barb yawned and checked her watch. "I am totally beat, and unlike you two I have a real job to get up for in the morning, so I'm going to bed."

When my glass was finally empty, I stood up and placed it on the coffee table. Wendy was stretched out on the sofa, eyes shut. I paused to admire the elegant curve of her hip visible in the gap between her t-shirt and her jeans before reaching down to gently take her glass and place it beside my own. Unable to find any blankets, I brushed the pizza crumbs off the cloth from the dining room table and spread it over her.

I was halfway out the door when she spoke. "We have to get them back, Jake."

"We will." I tried my best to make hope sound like confidence.

Wendy nodded without opening her eyes. "Good night."

Chapter Thirty-eight

The minute I turned my phone on the next morning, it began convulsing from a barrage of messages from the second recipient of my pre-yachting text. There was little variation in the repetitive imperative that had forced me to turn it off the night before so I could get some sleep.

call me
call me asap
call me!!
call me dammit
call me call me call me

In my weakened, pre-coffee state, I caved and dialed.

"Hey, Nina," I croaked. My throat felt like I had downed an entire cactus the night before, rather than just a half bottle of tequila.

"You asshole!"

"I'll survive, thanks for asking. How are you?"

"Didn't you get my texts?"

"Yup, I got, let's see..." I took the phone away from my ear just as Nina served up another helping of profanity. "Nine of them."

"Why the hell didn't you call me last night?"

"Didn't you get *my* text? I went out to Mickey Wu's boat. I didn't get home until really late."

"Oh, is that right? Because Mickey Wu got home at ten-thirty p.m."

I sat up in bed. "Is he still there?"

"No. According to Agent Chung, he left almost immediately in some kind of monster truck driven by some kind of monster. So you could have let my uncle's agents into the house last night after all."

I had little doubt that the "monster" was The Norwegian. They must have taken the Zodiac back to Mickey Wu's waterfront mansion. But if they didn't stay, it was a solid bet that Dante and Richard weren't there, either. I wondered where they might have gone. And whether Mickey Wu had enjoyed Dimmu Borgir. My guess was that symphonic black metal probably wasn't his thing, but people can sometimes surprise you.

"My uncle is furious with you."

"Furious enough to make you call the cops?"

Silence. Followed by the right answer. "No."

I yawned expansively. "Good. In that case, you can tell him I'm ready to help him out now. I'll come by your office in an hour to discuss the details."

"That's great, Jake. Thank you. This really is important to my uncle. And to me." The enthusiasm in her voice bothered me. Maybe because she had a very different tone, and attitude, when discussing my criminal tendencies in the past. "So we'll…"

"And I didn't find Richard and Dante. In case you were wondering."

I hung up without finding out if she had been.

Chapter Thirty-nine

I was beginning to miss Li Wei's scowl. At the moment he was smiling at me. Or a bit constipated. Possibly both. His upper lip remained stiff as Tupperware but the lower one sagged like a hammock to reveal a row of dental stalactites eroded far beyond the restorative powers of Colgate. At least his onyx eyes hadn't lost their sparkle. The man did have nice eyes. But I suspected that nothing that mouth did was ever going to make me happy.

"I will help you," it said.

Instead of gratitude, I only felt hungover. Or maybe it was the company I was keeping, rather than the noble agave plant, that was to blame for my nauseous state.

I averted my eyes from Li Wei's rictus of pleasure to take in the far more attractive features of his niece. Nina was also busily avoiding eye contact with her uncle. She did so by staring at her desk, where he was sitting. It was an oval expanse of red-tinted glass set atop chrome legs in the form of Xs. Li Wei drummed his manicured nails on its surface.

Tick, tick, tick, tick… Tick, tick, tick, tick… Tick, tick, tick, tick…

I tried to stop myself from going squirrelly by focusing on the office art, but it was office-art bland. I stared out the expansive windows, but the view of the expansive parking lot made the art look good. I considered dropping down to do a few push-ups on the wall-matching seafoam green carpet, but its off-gassing was worse than Li Wei's.

Defeated, I scowled at his claws with annoyance. They were of a distinctly feminine length, which explained the noise, and as worn and cracked as his chompers. The desktop, on the other hand, was crack-free.

I frowned at Nina. "Did you get a new desk?"

Her cheeks coloured as she met my gaze. "Yes."

She flashed me a hot-chilly smile. "I couldn't keep the old one, Jake. It wasn't safe."

I stared at her until she looked away. The crack in her old desk had been a meaningful faultline in our seismically active past. It had occurred during, or possibly slightly before, Nina's orgasm the last time I was in her office, several eons ago.

Li Wei yanked me back to the present, and further away from his niece. "When is your appointment at the bank?"

It took me a second to recall why he cared—Agent Wang would be coming with me. After which, I would accompany him to Mickey Wu's house, in the vicinity of which Agent Chung apparently continued to lurk. I would let them in, using Mickey Wu's door and alarm codes so they could do whatever it was they were planning—search it, trash it, even throw another party, for all I cared.

"Haven't made one yet," I replied, my mind back on who wanted to screw me now. "I need to get a fake ID first."

Agent Wang steepled his hands, tapping the tips of his fingers together rapidly. "Mickey Wu hasn't yet returned home yet, but he could at anytime. Mr. Constable may not be ready to proceed, but we are. I suggest we search Wu's house first, and deal with Mr. Constable's problem afterwards."

He was looking at Li Wei as he spoke, but I was damn sure going to have the final word on this. I knew there was zero chance of Agent Wang risking his ass if they didn't need me anymore. "No way. I'm not helping you until you've helped me."

Li Wei and Agent Wang proceeded to have a rapid exchange in Mandarin, after which Li Wei nodded. Agent Wang looked over at me. "Would one of your provincial driver's licences suffice as identification?"

Agent Wang had finally dropped the ingratiating smile, which made me suspect he was serious. I shrugged. "Yup, should."

The smile reappeared. "It can be ready in an hour. What name should be on it?"

Until that moment things had been coming together so nicely. When I had first mentioned the safety deposit box, Li Wei and Agent Wang had surprised me by not even asking whose it was. All that seemed to matter to them was that I would get them into Mickey Wu's house. Our mutual lack of interest in each other's nefarious doings had suited all parties perfectly. But now this.

Agent Wang was leaning over Nina's desk, pen poised over paper. Nina and Li Wei were staring at me expectantly, one might even say impatiently.

"Zhang Tao," I mumbled at last. There was no backing out now. My mind was racing to come up with a possible explanation for why I wanted to break into a safety deposit box belonging to a missing agent from the Chinese Ministry of Public Security.

Could I convince them that I was a deep cover Chinese sleeper agent auditing the Ministry's operational efficiencies? Unlikely. Maybe I could say I was doing an end run around them to liberate my friends while simultaneously luring Mickey Wu into the open to entangle him in a well-documented web of illegal activities so Agents Wang and Chung could swoop in and heroically bring him to justice and salvage the Ministry's reputation in the wake of a blackmail scandal involving one of its agents. It sounded a bit farfetched, but seemed like my best chance at bringing this thing home.

"Z... H... A... N... G... T... A... O. Is that correct, Mr. Constable?" Agent Wang asked without looking up.

Li Wei and Nina were conversing quietly in Mandarin, ignoring us both.

Dumbfounded, I scanned and verified their disinterest. "Uh...yeah. Yes, that's correct."

Agent Wang nodded. "I'll need to see a copy of the signature."

"Hold on." I pulled up the photo of Zhang Tao's ID on my phone, slowly putting a few more pieces together as I did. Zhang Tao's licence had to be as fake as the one Agent Wang was about to produce. As fake as the name Zhang Tao.

Before showing the photo to Agent Wang, I zoomed in on it until the signature on the licence filled the screen, leaving none of his colleague's photo visible. He studied it for a moment and then returned his attention to the pad of paper on the desk and began to practice the signature. Three tries and he had it down perfectly. Agent Wang smiled with evident professional pride. I couldn't blame him.

Chapter Forty

Agent Wang looked cool as a sea cucumber as he sat in the bank's waiting area browsing through a brochure on retirement savings funds. I was sweating like a stevedore. Partly it was nerves but mostly it was because of the quilted jacket I was wearing in spite of the day's balmy weather. I had chosen it for the large hidden pocket sewn into the lining of the jacket, used in the past to mule around shrink-wrapped packages of Granddad's Ganja, but today filled by a thick envelope of glossy 8x10s printed off of *beaversandbananas.com*, an explicit photo sharing website I had discovered a few hours earlier. Who knew amateur porn was such a popular form of creative expression? I sure wished I still didn't.

The embarrassment factor for the photos was already sky-high by any objective standard, but when I called the bank I hedged my bets by making our appointment with a woman named Dorothy Bernbaum rather than her more worldly sounding colleague, Maury Rogers.

"Mr. Tao?"

Agent Wang looked up from his brochure and smiled. I turned and joined him. Jackpot. Standing before us in a dusky-rose pantsuit was my old Sunday school teacher's stunt double. "I'm Mrs. Bernbaum," she cooed, hands clasped before her in the ready-to-pray position. She had a gossamer bouffant and kind eyes shyly peering out from beneath crinkly old eyelids gunked with makeup purchased in a bygone era of clearly defined genders and ramrod moral compasses. I knew instantly that this woman firmly believed beavers should be dammed and preferred her bananas on sundaes. Her angelic smile glowed as the fluorescent lights glanced off lipstick the colour of an overripe peach.

"Would you care to follow me?"

Agent Wang and I rose from our chairs. There was a soft clacking sound as Mrs. Bernbaum daintily raised the glasses hanging on a chain around her neck and slid them into place on the bridge of her nose. "And you are?"

"Jake Constable, ma'am. I'm with Mr. Tao."

She nodded and patted me on the arm. "Please do make yourself comfortable in our waiting area and we'll be back shortly. Right this way, Mr. Tao."

"Actually, if you don't mind, I'll just come along."

Mrs. Bernbaum wrinkled her nose. "Are you a registered co-renter of Mr. Tao's safety deposit box?"

"No, ma'am. But Mr. Tao invited me to join him." I reached out to place a friendly hand on Agent Wang's shoulder. "We're close friends."

"Isn't that nice." Mrs. Bernbaum gave me a reassuring smile before turning to Agent Wang. "I'm sorry but your friend will have to wait here. Our security policy stipulates that only registered renters may access the safety deposit boxes—I'm sure you understand."

Agent Wang nodded. "No problem."

"Yes, problem!"

Agent Wang and Mrs. Bernbaum looked over at me in surprise.

"I need to go with you, Mr. Tao. You…wanted my opinion on the documents, remember?" I forced a laugh. "I can't very well do that sitting out here, now can I? Mrs. Bernbaum, you said it was bank policy to only allow renters to access the boxes, and a policy is really just a guideline, isn't it? Surely exceptions can be made."

"Goodness me, is that what I said?" Mrs. Bernbaum put her hand to her mouth as if preparing to blow me a kiss. "I'm very sorry for the confusion. I actually I misspoke when I said that was the bank's security policy."

I smiled with relief. "No need to apologize. But we are in a bit of a rush so if…"

"What I meant to say was 'rule,'" Mrs. Bernbaum continued in the same carbide tone of voice my old Sunday School teacher had employed for the invocation of divine law and other forms of behaviour modification. "So are you going to drop your keister into that chair like a good little soldier, or do I need to have Mr. Edwards come over here to explain our security procedures to you?" She pointed toward a half-asleep Don Rickles impersonator in a rent-a-cop uniform.

"No, ma'am." I didn't want to be responsible for anyone's cardiac arrest. I already had enough cadavers on my conscience.

"I will take care of the documents myself," Agent Wang said with a smile as he followed after Mrs. Bernbaum toward her office. "Do not worry."

My pocket bulging with dirty pictures, I dropped my keister into the chair like a good little soldier and began to worry. It was Sunday School all over again.

Chapter Forty-one

I kept one eye on the door of the bank and the other on fake Don Rickles. After ten minutes I stopped worrying about the nonagenarian security guard making trouble, since he had begun snoring audibly. I also decided that more than enough time had passed for Mrs. Bernbaum to have alerted the authorities if Agent Wang had failed to convince her that he was Zhang Tao, so I stopped worrying about the cops charging through the door.

Which freed me up to worry about other things. Like what Agent Wang was going to do once he got a look at the information on Mickey's daughter. Ditching me seemed to be a likely option. I assumed Agents Wang and Chung wanted to search Mickey Wu's place to find something that would give them the leverage to force him to return to China. Both Zhang Tao and Mickey Wu seemed to think that the documents in the safety deposit box would do the trick, and who was I to doubt their expertise in the matter? So, once Agent Wang had them, he would probably lose interest in breaking into Mickey Wu's house. Which meant he wouldn't need me anymore.

The credibility of my hypothesis increased when I spotted Mrs. Bernbaum return to her office without Agent Wang.

I hurried over and barged in just as she was closing the door. "Where's Agent...my, uh, real estate agent, Mr. Tao?"

Mrs. Bernbaum exhaled gassily. "You're a very rude young man, aren't you?"

"Yes, ma'am."

She pursed her lips and glanced at her phone.

"If you're thinking of calling for Don Rickles, don't bother. He's having his nap. I'm sorry for barging in like this. It's just that Mr. Tao and I are on the verge of closing a killer deal and time is very much of the essence. Is he still back with the safety deposit boxes?"

She looked aghast. "I certainly wouldn't leave him there by himself. The bank's security rules prohibit…"

I waved my hands in surrender. "I'm sure they do. So where is he, then?"

Mrs. Bernbaum hummed to herself for a moment. "I don't know why I should tell you anything. Are you even a client of this bank?"

I nodded earnestly. "Ever since my dad opened a junior saver account for me on my seventh birthday. Just before his heart attack," I added haltingly, as if in the grips of an emotion.

Her eyes narrowed. "There's no such thing as a junior saver account."

"Fine. Listen, I promise I'll leave as soon as you answer my question. I really am in a hurry."

Mrs. Bernbaum huffed twice before squeezing around behind her desk and dropping her pant-suited derriere into the chair. She arranged her reading glasses on her nose and affected great interest in a stack of forms in front of her. "After Mr. Tao was finished with his deposit box he very politely excused himself and went to visit the little boy's room."

"Thanks. And when you're finished looking at those, have a gander at these." I took the manila envelope from my bag and tossed it on her desk. "Maybe you'll recognize some clients."

Chapter Forty-two

Mrs. Bernbaum took the Lord's name in vain loud enough to wake fake Don Rickles from his slumber. Out of the corner of my eye, I saw him reach her office just as I reached the john. I didn't really expect to find Agent Wang there but I had to go through the motions.

After ensuring that both the facilities and my bladder were empty, I decided to bug out before Mrs. Bernbaum found the section of the policy manual pertaining to the circulation of the bank's revenue reports and other obscene materials. On my way out, I saw her standing outside her office conferring quietly with a portly man with salt-and-pepper hair and an expression of solemn concern. Her expression of mortification curdled into something nasty when she spotted me. I quickened my pace accordingly.

I had initially been relieved to see that the security guard hadn't been part of the huddle but felt less sanguine when I spotted him loitering near the door. Worse yet, he started moving toward it as I approached.

Fake Don Rickles arrived at the exit one step ahead of me and reached out to grab the door handle.

"Thanks, I got it." Before he had a chance to say anything I gave the door a hard shove. It pulled him off balance, forcing him to let go before he toppled over entirely. I was outside in an instant and heading around the corner at a jog. I heard an angry "Hey!" behind me but didn't turn.

On most days I wouldn't change a single thing on the Porsche 911 but at that moment I would've traded it for a Ford Fiesta if it came with a fob. I had the key in the door and was watching the lock pop up when I felt the arm around my neck. I wouldn't have credited fake Don Rickles with the strength or the technique to spin me around like a top until it started to happen a split second later.

"Watch the bodywork," I grunted as I was slammed onto the hood. "This is a classic."

"Yes, it is." Agent Wang nodded slowly as he looked it over. "And I thought we agreed that you were going to take me for a ride in it."

I grinned up at him. "It would be my pleasure."

"Then why were you trying to ditch me?"

Over Agent Wang's shoulder, through the window of the bank, I could see Mrs. Bernbaum staring at us as she fanned herself with a term deposit brochure. She was flanked by a surly looking fake Don Rickles and the portly salt-and-pepper banker, who merely looked perplexed. I nevertheless felt satisfied that we had officially worn out our welcome. "Did you get the documents?"

"Of course," Agent Wang replied indignantly.

"Great." I climbed off the hood of the car. "Jump in. I'll try to explain on the way."

Chapter Forty-three

"So where the hell did you disappear to?" My junior hockey coach always told me that the best defence is a good offence.

Agent Wang was suitably taken aback. "I had to stop by the restroom to do a number two."

I looked over at him appraisingly. "You know your use of idiom is very impressive."

Once again he beamed with professional pride so I decided to switch gears. "And I wasn't trying to ditch you—I thought *you* had ditched *me* when Mrs. Bernbaum returned without you. I went into her office to ask where you had gone. She said you had gone to the bathroom but by the time I checked it you must have been done."

Agent Wang nodded. "When I came out, you were no longer in the waiting area, so I exited the bank and found a discrete location to wait and watch your car. It is unwise to linger at the scene of a crime."

I couldn't disagree with him there. "So where are the documents?"

He popped the locks on his briefcase and extracted an envelope. I was pleasantly surprised to note two things: First, it was still sealed. Second, it was identical to the ringer I had left with Mrs. Bernbaum. It was reassuring to see that the entire plan hadn't been terrible.

"Slow down."

I reflexively checked the road ahead and the rearview mirrors but didn't see any cops. "Why? What's the problem?"

"I just received a text from my partner. Mickey Wu has returned home."

I hit the gas. "Is anyone with him?"

Agent Wang shook his head. "I said *slow down*. We have to wait until he leaves before we go in. And he knows you, so I don't want him to see us near his house. It might arouse his suspicions."

"But we could follow him. Don't you think it's weird he didn't come home last night? We might be able to find out where he's staying." I was confident that wherever it was, I would find Richard and Dante there as well.

Agent Wang managed to hiss primly. "Most likely with one of his girlfriends. He spends an average of four nights a week at their various residences."

"Impressive."

"Degenerate," Agent Wang replied scornfully.

"I didn't mean Mickey Wu. I'm talking about you and Agent Chung. You guys really do your homework."

Agent Wang inclined his head modestly. "Thank you. But do not try to 'butter me up.'" He tried but failed to suppress a grin. "Do as I say and decelerate immediately. I fulfilled my end of our deal, no questions asked. Now it is time for you to fulfill yours."

I cursed and slammed on the brakes. Not because of Agent Wang's appeal to my sense of honour but to avoid slamming into the car ahead of me on the Burrard Street Bridge. Traffic was bumper-to-bumper as usual, and there was no avoiding it. Zhang Tao had done his banking downtown whereas Mickey Wu lived in Kitsilano, on the other side of False Creek. I had never been sure whether Vancouver was intruding into the ocean or the other way around. It made for lots of dramatic coastline and nice views, but also meant you usually had to cross a bridge just to go to the bathroom.

"But you don't know for sure he was at his girlfriend's place, right? What if he's about to leave town? Maybe he knows you're after him."

"How could he know that?" Agent Wang studied me suspiciously. "Have you spoken with him?"

I kept my eyes on the road. "Mickey Wu fired me before I even met you. But I was his house-sitter and let me tell you, the guy is a real jetsetter. I wouldn't want you to lose track of him."

Agent Wang said nothing. He had a heck of a poker face so I had no idea whether he was considering what I said or had simply decided to ignore me entirely. In any event, gridlock traffic was accomplishing the goal of stopping me from getting to Mickey Wu's place anytime soon.

"We can't make contact with Mr. Wu until we have more information," Agent Wang said at last.

"You mean leverage, right?" I glanced over at him. "To force him to return to China."

"Our objective is to convince him to return home voluntarily. To make reparations for his crimes."

I didn't bother to respond. We had reached the far side of the bridge, which rendered the nuances of Operation Fox Hunt, and my deal with Agent Wang, moot points, as far as I was concerned. I nosed my way onto the Cornwall exit and goosed the 911 toward Point Grey Road, now only minutes away.

To my surprise, Agent Wang didn't complain. He was busy reading another text. "We are fine. Mr. Wu is leaving now."

Agent Wang groaned when yet another text chimed in.

"What's the matter now?"

"Mr. Wu has a suitcase with him."

Chapter Forty-four

We spent the rest of the short ride in a funk. Agent Wang was worried that his quarry really might be preparing to leave town. Personally, I wasn't concerned about the suitcase. I knew there was no way Mickey Wu was going anywhere without the documents on his daughter. My guess was that he had returned home to pick up a change of thongs and was now headed back to wherever he had Richard and Dante stashed—and I had just missed the opportunity to find out where that was.

Agent Wang motioned for me to pull in behind a blue Chevy Impala with tinted windows parked a half block down the street from Mickey Wu's wall of bamboo. "Come on," he said.

As soon as we got out of the car, Agent Chung emerged from the Impala. I waved at him. "What's shaking?"

He paused, frowning. "I do not believe anything is."

"He does not understand idiom," Agent Wang whispered to me as we walked toward him.

"So you're saying it's all Greek to him?" I whispered back.

Agent Wang giggled. "Yes, with Agent Chung it is all jumbo mumbo."

I nudged him with my elbow. "Great minds think alike." His smile withered when he noticed Agent Chung glaring at us. They went back and forth in Mandarin for a couple minutes, after which Agent Chung appeared mollified. "Okay, let's go," he said. "Time is…wasting?"

Agent Wang nodded encouragingly. I reached over and slapped him on the shoulder. "Now you're getting it."

It had occurred to me that Mickey Wu might have changed his codes after my festive misadventures in his abode so it was a relief when I entered the sequence of numbers on the door panel and heard the deadbolt thunk back into its cylinder. When I pushed Mickey Wu's front door open, it was pure adrenaline rush. Not just because of the view, which was still spectacular. Nor because the alarm immediately began to whine ominously. The rush came from the pure thrill of entering the house illegally.

If Agents Wang and Chung were also feeling the buzz, they didn't show it. As soon as I silenced the alarm, they calmly strode into the house with a clear sense of purpose. One might almost think they had done this kind of thing before.

Having no sense of purpose of my own, I decided to return to the scene of the crime. "I gotta drop some friends off at the pool," I called after them and beelined for the bathroom.

I knew Mickey Wu would have had it cleaned up, but it still felt strange to be standing in that gleaming, lemon-scented bathroom knowing that a man had so recently been lying there, slowly decomposing in a puddle of his own blood. It also gave me a feeling of satisfaction to picture Thaddeus down on his knees mopping it up.

Having already made a deposit at the bank, I gave the toilet a flush for effect and went to look for the secret agents.

I found them in the kitchen. Agent Chung had rolled up his sleeves and replaced his suit coat with an apron. He was chopping up bok choy with blinding speed and tossing it into a sizzling wok. The air was fragrant with garlic and sesame. All I could say was, "Wow."

He ignored me but Agent Wang retracted his head from

Mickey Wu's wine fridge and nodded. "Chung used to be a chef." He stood up with a bottle of Pinot Grigio and began rummaging through drawers.

I pointed to the wine opener mounted on the slate countertop at the far end of the kitchen. "Far be it from me to call anyone unprofessional, but I thought you guys were here to search this place."

"After lunch," Agent Chung grunted.

Agent Wang gestured for me to grab some wineglasses from the wall-mounted rack beside me. "It's a beautiful day. Shall we eat outside?"

●● ● ●●

"The steamed trout is incredible." I helped myself to another glass of Mickey Wu's wine, which was also excellent. We were seated around the table on Mickey Wu's deck overlooking the ocean. The low angle of the autumn sunshine was almost blinding. "Is that ginger I'm tasting?"

Agent Chung continued to stare out at the Pacific but I could see that he was smiling. "It is."

"So what's a talented chef like you doing in a mansion like this?"

"I used to work in a very nice restaurant in Shanghai but it closed down." Agent Chung shrugged. "I needed a new job. My father and brother are policemen, so I joined the..." he looked at me shyly, "...family business?"

I gave him a thumbs-up.

"That is not the whole story," said Agent Wang. "Chung was not just the chef but also the owner of the restaurant. And it was very popular, very successful. But he refused to pay money to the local Party Secretary, so it was closed down for health violations. All fabricated, of course, but his reputation was ruined." He glanced at Agent Chung. "After that, no one would hire him as a chef."

I looked over at Agent Chung as well but he had resumed staring out at the ocean, his expression unreadable. "Well, I'm glad you still get a chance to spend time in the kitchen, even if it is Mickey Wu's. Your boss doesn't mind you doing this? Or does he not know?"

Agent Wang looked confused. "Our boss?"

"Li Wei."

Agent Chung's head snapped around. "That man is *not* our boss."

"Whoa, didn't mean to offend you guys. I thought he was running the show but clearly I made a mistake." Agent Chung's comment, and the vehemence with which he delivered it, raised them both in my estimation. I decided to try and have an open mind, assuming the hinges weren't already rusted shut.

"We don't work for him, but Li Wei is a high-ranking member of the Party and does have...a lot of influence," Agent Wang said carefully.

"Yeah, I read up on him a bit. Seems like he's pretty good at getting his name in the news. Particularly when it comes to corruption initiatives."

"*Anti*-corruption," Agent Chung corrected, scowling. In this, at least, he and Li Wei were on the same page.

I raised a placating hand. "I know, Operation Fox Hunt is all about you super spies going around nailing corrupt bigwigs..."

Agent Chung looked confused until Agent Wang provided what I assumed to be an appropriate Mandarin translation.

"But from what I read, Li Wei was one of the foxes before he became a hunter."

The super spies exchanged a look.

"He was the subject of a corruption probe a number of years ago," Agent Wang allowed. "But never convicted of anything. Since then, Li Wei has been a vocal proponent of anti-corruption initiatives, including Operation Fox Hunt. Though he has no official connection to it."

"You mean he's not on your list?"

This elicited a sardonic smile from Agent Chung. "Not at the moment."

"So I guess the squeaky wheel isn't getting greased. Colour me surprised."

This time, both of my lunch companions looked mystified. "Forget it," I said with a dismissive wave. "So if he's not actually part of Operation Fox Hunt, why is he calling the shots?"

"It is…unusual for a senior Party member to take such interest in low-level field operations such as ours."

Unsatisfied with Agent Wang's non-answer, I re-framed the question. "Is he here to cover his own ass?"

He began to translate this into Mandarin but Agent Chung cut him off. "Yes," he said bitterly.

"Because Mickey Wu is Nina's client?"

"A client of Blue Coast Realty," Agent Chung corrected. "An agency co-owned by Li Wei and your ex-wife."

I opened my mouth then closed it again. This was news to me. I knew that Nina's uncle had been responsible for referring some of her wealthier clients but she had never mentioned they were partners. No wonder she checked her backbone at the door every time he was in the room.

"So let me guess: as soon as Li Wei found out that Nina's client was on your list, he parachuted in to personally bring Mickey Wu to justice, thereby demonstrating to the other Party bigwigs that Li Wei was all about putting the 'anti' back into his corruption initiatives."

The super spies nodded in unison. "He actually arrived by private jet," Agent Chung said. "But, yes, the rest of your summation is accurate. Several people on the Ministry's list are believed to be here in Vancouver. We were working on different targets but the agent responsible for Mickey Wu had apparently made no progress and is now missing. When Li Wei contacted the Ministry to report Mr. Wu's whereabouts and express personal interest in bringing him to justice, we were reassigned to assist him."

I was relieved to hear that Agents Wang and Chung weren't Li Wei's flunkies because I was actually starting to like them. It was a hard thing to admit since they were in law enforcement, but I took some solace in the fact that they were going after the power brokers who were rigging the game against the rest of us. Which meant it had to really chafe to be kowtowing to Li Wei while he whitewashed his reputation. I decided to forgive them for being standoffish when we first met.

It also made me want to help them nail some corrupt bigwigs. Li Wei, ideally. Or at least Mickey Wu. Despite having recently been fired, however, the last thing I wanted was more work. I was having a hard enough time taking care of the job at hand, getting Richard and Dante back.

"Time to get to work," said Agent Wang.

I offered to do the dishes. After all the hospitality Mickey Wu had inadvertently shown me, cleaning up seemed like the right thing to do. Especially if it would prevent Mickey from knowing that I had been in his house again.

Chapter Forty-five

When I was finished in the kitchen, I wandered through the house, coming across Agents Chung and Wang hard at work in Mickey's office. I watched them for a moment, trying to imagine what they might be looking for. Then I remembered I had it in my shoulder bag.

After ducking out and fetching my bag from the car, I checked to make sure the super spies were still occupied. Agent Chung was performing some kind of delicate operation on a recalcitrant safe and Agent Wang was totally engrossed by what he was doing on or to Mickey Wu's computer. I doubted he was poking around *beaversandbananas.com*, but whatever he was into was probably even more invasive than what I had seen on that website.

I went into Mickey Wu's bedroom, flopped onto his king-sized pillowtop, and opened the envelope.

The photos were much more tasteful than the ones I left with Mrs. Bernbaum, notwithstanding the stalker vibe they gave off. I spread them out beside me on the bed. There were several of Mickey Wu and his daughter on various father-daughter outings—having brunch, shopping for clothes, having lunch, coming out of an art gallery, having dinner (for a guy with such a nice kitchen, he seemed to eat out a lot, but at least he put in the time with his kid). I recognized a couple of local landmarks, so clearly she had come to town to visit him, which might have been how Agent Zhang found out about her. There were also a number of photos of her without Mickey, which must have been taken down at Stanford. In these she was surrounded by fresh-faced, intelligent, optimistic-looking people her own age, many wearing backpacks with plastic bottles like Wendy's clipped to them. In one she was walking down a sidewalk past a low wall with the words "Graduate School of Business" and "Stanford University" on it.

In addition to the pictures, there was a sheet of paper stating that her name was Cynthia Chang and provided her address. Zhang Tao had also prepared a detailed log of the girl's visit to Vancouver in late August, during which she had stayed with Mickey. The final items in the envelope were a copy of her current class schedule and three tuition receipts from Stanford made out to Mickey Wu. Taken together, the photographs and the accompanying documents comprised an excellent roadmap leading right to Mickey Wu's daughter.

I looked through the photos again. In the ones with Mickey, Cynthia's expression was difficult to read—she seemed restrained but not unhappy (the painfully tight-looking pony-tail she invariably pulled her hair back into might've been partially to blame). Mickey, by contrast, looked more animated than I had ever seen him. Not that we had spent much time together, or under circumstances conducive to warm feelings. But that's what he emanated when he was with his daughter. Not just affection, but also pride. Which might have something to do with the second set of pictures, the ones taken at Stanford. There, Cynthia seemed totally at ease. In some she was laughing; in others, earnest and thoughtful. In all of them, her gaze was arrestingly intense, her brown eyes shining with a canny intelligence—in this sole aspect she evoked her father almost perfectly. She looked younger than she must be, particularly in the ones where she had loosely braided her hair into long pigtails, though in most she simply let it hang loose.

In aggregate, the Stanford photos painted a picture of a bright, well-adjusted young woman filled with enthusiasm and very much in her element. I never would have guessed she was the daughter of a sleazebag like Mickey Wu if he hadn't told me so himself. I couldn't blame Mickey for wanting to keep Cynthia, and the life she was making for herself at Stanford, hidden and protected from the reach of the Chinese government.

"What are those?"

I looked up to find Agent Chung standing in the doorway watching me. "Jeez, you startled me." I spoke loudly so he could hear me over the bass drum that was suddenly hammering away in my chest. The resulting surge in blood flow made it hard to act casual as I hastily crammed the photos back into envelope. "I guess sneaking up on people is Spycraft 101."

Agent Chung said nothing, possibly because he was still waiting for an answer to his question. Apparently, being nosey was also Spycraft 101. "Just some stuff Agent Wang helped me retrieve from a safety-deposit box earlier."

"They are not Mickey Wu's?"

"Nope." Which was technically true for the time being. Mickey Wu's face grinned up at me affectionately as the last photo slid into the envelope.

Agent Chung studied me for another moment before nodding. "I need to search this room."

"You didn't find what you're looking for in the office?"

"Wang has made a copy of the computer hard drive. We may still find something on it. But no, nothing so far."

I hopped off the bed and beelined for the door, stepping around Agent Chung as he entered the room.

"Wait, please."

I turned to see Agent Chung pulling a picture out from

beneath the pillow I had smooshed up behind my back. A sly smile spread across his features as he examined the photo. "She is very pretty." He handed me the photo. "But much too young for you."

I grabbed the photo of Cynthia wearing a Stanford sweatshirt and stuffed it in my pocket with a laugh. "Middle-aged guy dates girl twenty years younger. Quick, call CNN."

Chapter Forty-six

Once I was alone in the kitchen I pulled the picture of Cynthia out of my pocket and returned it to the envelope with the rest. Then I raided Mickey Wu's fridge in search of something to replace the guilty feeling in my gut. I would've liked to help Agents Wang and Chung but I needed the info on Mickey Wu's daughter to bargain for the safe return of Richard and Dante. Truth be told, putting her on the board in Mickey Wu's chess match with the Chinese government didn't sit right anyway. Maybe Barb's lecture on parents and kids not suffering for each other's mistakes (okay, crimes) had hit home after all.

By the time I had finished my second bowl of Chocolate Cherry Garcia, the super spies were ready to go. Mickey Wu must've been doing a good job of keeping his affairs in order because their mood was glum as they conversed in Mandarin. Having nothing I was willing to offer, I silently waited by the front door. Until they seemed to briefly switch to Norwegian. "Wait a minute, what did you just say?"

Agent Wang looked over me with an expression of faint annoyance. "We are just shop talking."

"You mean talking shop," I said helpfully, if unwisely, as his annoyance ticked up a couple notches. "You just said something that wasn't Mandarin. I think it might have been Norwegian?"

He looked perplexed for a moment. "Dimmu Borgir?" he said at last.

"That's it, yes. I didn't peg you guys as heavy metal fans."

Agent Wang put his hands on his hips. "What are you talking about?"

"What are *you* talking about?" I countered.

"Mickey Wu's affairs, I told you."

"So he's the metal fan? Wouldn't have guess that either."

The super spies now looked more interested than confused. "Are you familiar with this corporation?"

"Unfortunately, yes. But it's not a corporation. Dimmu Borgir is a symphonic black metal band from Oslo."

The super spies reverted to looking more confused than interested.

"Oslo." I repeated. "It's the capital of Norway." If symphonic black metal was what was troubling them, all I could offer was membership to the club.

"We know what Oslo is," Agent Chung snapped. "But this Dimmu Borgir that Mickey Wu owns is not from there."

"Mickey Wu *owns* Dimmu Borgir? Wow, he really is building quite the eclectic empire." As improbable as it sounded, it would at least explain why The Norwegian was such a fan of Mickey Wu's.

"Mickey Wu is a shareholder. But not the majority owner," Agent Wang said by way of clarification, though it failed to make things any clearer for me.

The stench of lunacy was all around us now. Eyes narrowed as private suspicions festered on which among us was to blame. I waved an olive branch, hoping to clear the air. "I think you guys might be barking up the wrong tree here. Mickey Wu has been hanging out with a guy who is seriously into that band, but it wouldn't have anything to do with his business affairs."

"We are certain it does. Copies of the incorporation documents and share certificates were in his file cabinet," Agent Wang replied.

None of this was making any sense. "Show me."

• • ● • •

The incorporation documents certainly looked pedantic enough to be genuine. It had been a bit hard to believe when he told me about it back at his grow op, but maybe The Norwegian really was trying to go straight after all. And, most surprising of all, Mickey Wu had apparently invested in the company.

"Now I get it. Dimmu Borgir, Inc. is a real estate development company."

Agent Wang was still reading the Wikipedia page on Dimmu Borgir with an incredulous expression, but Agent Chung was paying close attention. "How can you be certain of this?" he asked.

I tapped the document. "I know The Norwegian."

Agent Chung looked nonplussed.

"He's the other shareholder," I explained. "And his fondest dream is to build condos."

"Dark fortresses," Agent Wang murmured.

I glanced at him uncertainly. "I guess you could call them that…particularly if The Norwegian designs them himself."

"That is what Dimmu Borgir means," he elaborated, looking up from the monitor.

"Ah. That explains why The Norwegian named the company after his favourite band—it works on as many levels as he does. But I don't think it reveals anything about the corporate ethos. Property development can be a bit of a sleazy racket, I grant you, but it's not illegal. Sorry, guys."

The super spies looked disappointed, and I couldn't blame them. "What about these other files?" I pulled out a thick one but its contents were in Mandarin.

"That is a list of assets owned by one of Wu's companies back in China. We already have all that information. Some of the assets are of suspicious origin, but it doesn't matter. We need evidence of criminal activities here in Canada."

"I thought you guys were after him for what he did back home," I said as I flipped through the file. Most of the pages were filled with text but there were also photos of a couple of fancy-looking houses on white sand beaches, a mid-sized hotel in Manhattan, and even a yacht I recognized—*The Chairman.*

"Yes, but without an extradition treaty in place, Canada will not surrender him to face charges back in China. However, Mickey Wu does not have Canadian citizenship."

"So what? He's here legally, isn't he?"

"Of course. But if he commits a crime, your government will revoke his visa and deport him. Which is why we will be taking a close look at the activities of this Dimmu Borgir."

"Well, I wish you luck. If it's any help, I've been told that their best album was *Death Cult Armageddon.*"

Chapter Forty-seven

As I drove away from Mickey Wu's house, I found myself unable to get the concussive harangue of the lead guitar line from The Norwegian's all-time favourite Dimmu Borgir track, "Progenies of the Great Apocalypse," out of my head. I chose to take it as an omen, along with two Advil, as soon as possible.

I had been feeling good about getting my hands on the documents I needed to get Richard and Dante back, but another problem now raised its mulleted head—The Norwegian would not take it well if the super spies found some irregularity in Dimmu Borgir, Inc. and used that to take Mickey Wu down. I had little doubt that my former business partner would blame me if anything happened to his current one.

I contemplated what proactive steps I could take beyond simply believing that The Norwegian was telling me the truth about going straight. The only idea that came to mind wasn't a particularly palatable one, but I had no choice. I pulled a U-turn and headed for Nina's office.

I leaned against the doorframe and put on a casual smile. "Hey, babe."

Nina winced at the sound of my voice. A couple minutes

after that, she looked up from her phone. It was just like being married again.

"Oh, God, Jake. Please tell me you didn't come back to renege on our deal again."

"Nope. Deal's already done. Agent Wang helped me get what I needed and I did the same for him and your uncle. In fact, it all went so well that I came by to see if you guys wanted to make another one."

"Do tell." Her expression seemed to request the opposite.

"I'd like to, but I think this one might be above your pay-grade. Is your uncle around?"

If looks could kill, I would've died a happy man.

"He's at his hotel taking a nap. I'm not about to disturb him unless you tell me what you could possibly have to offer him."

"A real estate deal, as it happens."

"Real estate…? Hello? What do you think I do around here?"

"To be honest, at this point I'm not really sure. Whatever it is, I assume you're probably on probation, thanks to this business with Mickey Wu. And right now I need someone who can take swift, executive action."

I needed the deal I had in mind more than they did. In fact, I suspected that Li Wei needed it like he needed a hole in the head. As much as I might like to give him one, the deal was all I had to offer. And I doubted he would even be interested in that. Which left Nina. The problem was, protecting Li Wei was very much in her self-interest, and few things in this world had a chance of overcoming a force that powerful. Her affection for me definitely wasn't one of them. But her ego just might be.

"*On probation?* That's, what, petty criminal humour? Very cute, but I really don't have time to goof around with you right now." Nina began fiddling with her phone, presumably since it was the only thing on her desk. "As you can see, I'm busy running a real estate agency here. Making actual deals for some of my wealthy clients. You remember them, right? The people you used to house-sit for?"

"I'm not goofing around here, Nina. I'm trying to save Richard and Dante's lives." Her fingers had gone still on her phone so I knew I was reaching her. Now I just needed to move past our vexation flirtations and touch her in a way that never failed to make her heart beat faster. "And make you a lot of money."

It took another half hour to fully equip her ego with the weaponry necessary to hijack her self-interest, but in the end Nina agreed to the deal I had in mind. Or rather, Blue Coast Realty agreed to the deal with Dimmu Borgir, Inc. Of course, it wouldn't be official until I got The Norwegian to sign on the dotted line, but that would be the easy part.

"I've got to say, Nina. I'm impressed. You really know your business."

She rolled her eyes. "You're only just figuring that out now? Did you forget that I got you fourteen thousand off the asking price on your loft?"

"Four thousand, actually. But the point is, I underestimated you and I apologize. And I know you're busy so I'll get out of your hair." I reached the doorway before snapping my fingers and turning back, trying my best to channel Peter Falk. "There's just one more thing—you're sure you don't need to run this by your uncle first?"

Nina bristled. "This is my agency, Jake. I don't need to ask anyone's permission to do a deal. I'm going to have my legal team draw up the paperwork right now."

I smiled and waved good-bye without another word.

Chapter Forty-eight

i have the docs. when and where?

8551 French Street first thing tomorrow.
Come alone.

see you then =)

Before pressing "send" I deleted the smiley face. I really can't stand emoticons.

Chapter Forty-nine

Wendy leaned on the table and tapped a finger on her chin as she added things up. "So let me see if I've got this straight: The narcissistic ex-wife cancels out the Viking ex-business partner, and the Chinese government agents are going to take care of the homicidal drug-peddling underwear salesman?"

"And the Communist Party power-broker, yes." I took another sip of San Luis del Rio. The earthy flavours of the Mezcal took their time sashaying across my tongue before hopping an express vein to my heart.

"Leaving us free to take Richard and Dante out on a double-date to celebrate their liberation." Wendy gestured to the dish in front of us. "Did you want that last taco al pastor?"

"Yes. And no. Help yourself." The tacos at La Mezcaleria on Commercial Drive were the best in the city but seven was my limit. "Wait a minute. Did you say 'us'?"

She nodded her head, her mouth already full of pork and pineapple.

I shook mine. "No way. Not us. Me. You remember the part about the Viking and the underwear salesman being homicidal, right?"

"And you remember my little friend here, right?"

I experienced a small, post-traumatic shudder at the sight of her stun gun, which had somehow appeared in her hand. "I recall being introduced. But you haven't met The Norwegian."

"I'm tougher than I look, Jake," she pressed. "Do you know how Dante and I first met?"

"Strata council meeting?"

"Try jujutsu class. I was his instructor."

"So you're…what, like a ninja or something?" I tried to remain calm, but it was hard because Wendy was seeming more and more like a real world manifestation of a comic book character I came up with when I was a kid. My ninja had actually been bisexual and used electrified nunchucks. She also did LSD rather than Ecstasy. But hey, it was an era of free love and psychedelics.

"That's ninjutsu, dummy. But I could still have you on the ground in about four seconds if I wanted to."

She'd get no argument there. Right before he went out to the drugstore on the other side of the world, my dad had given me his first and last piece of fatherly advice: don't ask questions you don't want to hear the answer to. But now, as then, the stakes were too high not to know the truth. "Are you messing with me right now?"

Wendy shook her head. "Scout's honour."

"Well, this does change things a bit," I allowed. Against my better judgment, I found myself considering taking her along. Which wasn't all that surprising since my better judgment was in the middle of a dry spell that started around the time I turned fourteen. After the way my last meeting with Mickey Wu turned out, I didn't hate the idea of having someone along to watch my back, not to mention Buff's well-muscled pair.

"I'm serious about this, Jake. I want to get Dante and Richard back just as much as you do. And let's be honest, you could use all the help you can get."

Even if she wasn't bisexual, my still heart raced with adolescent excitement at the thought of bringing along my very own ninja with her very own stun gun. "Okay, you've convinced me. I'll pick you up at nine a.m. tomorrow. Don't forget your little friend there."

"Not a chance. It goes wherever I go."

"Everywhere? Even the shower? Because that could be a bit dangerous."

Wendy patted my hand. "Many of the things I've done in the shower would probably shock you."

Chapter Fifty

"You should call your mom," Barb advised me.

"Thanks for the advice. I've actually got a bit of a busy morning planned but I could probably squeeze in a parental lecture after I rescue Richard and Dante." I handed Barb the coffee I now regretted buying as a peace offering and walked past her into the apartment.

She popped the lid and peered into the cup suspiciously. "I'm actually more of a tea drinker."

"Of course you are."

"But don't worry about it." The corners of her mouth started to elevate unevenly, like a jib cranked up on rusty lines for the first time after a long, wet winter.

"I wasn't." What was more concerning to me at the moment was her unprecedented attempt to smile at me.

"Seriously, Jake. Call to congratulate her."

"For what?"

Barb's look of surprise was fleeting. "You didn't know. Of course. Why would you? She's receiving the Transport Canada Certificate of Bravery! Isn't that exciting?"

"If you say so." It seemed politic to keep my doubts to myself at that moment.

"And it's sort of thanks to you."

"How so?" I was not at all sure I'd like the answer.

"Captain Constable is getting the award for seizing that boat with the drugs on it."

For a split second, my heart stopped. The only boat full of drugs I could think of that my mom had me to thank for was my grandfather's. But she couldn't be receiving an award for that one since that had happened years ago. And she hadn't seized it, a fact for which I was eternally grateful in my own non-showy way. Either out of maternal protectiveness or because she had been too busy cursing at me as we watched it sink beneath the waves. "You've lost me."

Barb's expression had become one of impatience. I knew exactly how she felt.

"You *do* remember that yacht where we rescued you from that hairbag thug the other night? The one that had all that opium on it?"

"I remember the yacht," I allowed carefully. "But what's this about opium?"

Barb grabbed a copy of yesterday's *Vancouver Sun* from the coffee table and thrust it at me. "It's been all over the news for the past couple days."

I scanned the story, on page one no less, honing in on the salient details as fast as I could since I really did have a busy morning lined up. My mother featured prominently, cast as the heroic Coast Guard captain who risked life and limb to seize a luxury yacht along with "an unidentified suspect," who I deduced was Thaddeus, since I was pretty sure they weren't talking about me. Upon searching the vessel, the police discovered almost two hundred kilos of opium with an estimated street value of eight million dollars.

"Pretty amazing, don't you think?" asked Barb eagerly.

"I do think. But it says here that the yacht was registered to a foreign corporation, 'whose ownership neither the police nor the media had thus far been able to determine.'" I looked up at her. "But we already know that Mickey Wu is the owner."

Assuming he read the paper more often than I did, it occurred to me that maybe Mickey's suitcase had been packed with more than a few thongs, after all.

Seeing Barb's expression, I wasted no time in clarifying my position. "Don't worry, I'm not going to tell the cops about Mickey Wu. Not while he still has Richard and Dante in hand and a chip on his shoulder. That's why I asked my mom to hide me below deck when the cops arrived to take custody of *The Chairman*. And I appreciate the risk she—and you—took in doing so ."

Barb crossed her arms. "Well…good."

"She's even getting a nice award out of the deal. Sounds like a happy ending to me."

"Except for the fact that Mickey Wu is a drug-smuggler," Barb shot back indignantly. "How is it a happy ending if he gets away with that?"

I patted my pockets for a notebook. "Would it make you feel any better if I added 'catch the drug-smuggler' to my to-do list right below 'rescue Richard and Dante'? Or did you still want me to call my mom before I take care of all that?"

Chapter Fifty-one

My illuminating encounter with Barb had put us behind schedule so I was relieved to find Wendy ready to go, though secretly disappointed that she wasn't dressed like a ninja. At least she was packing her stun gun, as promised.

We were at Nina's office twenty minutes later, thanks to light traffic and plentiful parking. Such driving conditions occurred in Vancouver about as often as getting sideswiped by a unicorn, and I couldn't decide whether to take them as auspicious omens or signs of an approaching apocalypse.

My feeling of unease only grew as I eased into a spot in front of the Blue Coast Realty office that still had forty minutes on the meter. "I need to run in and pick something up. You want to wait in the car?"

"And miss my chance to meet the woman who wanted to marry you?" Wendy shook her head. "Not on your life."

"She also divorced me, so you may be disappointed by her apparent level of lunacy."

Our entrance into the office was an emotional rollercoaster—I was dismayed that Li Wei was there, but pleased to see the secret agents. "How's it hanging, guys?"

"Long and loose and full of juice." Agent Chung followed up with a grin, which, under the circumstances, I found inordinate. "I have been researching idiom on the Internet," he added by way of explanation.

"Right...well, keep at it." I surveyed the room and its occupants, hoping to extract a core sample of the general vibe. Of note was the fact that Nina had kicked off the factory-worker stompers and replaced them with her favourite pair of John Fluevogs. Footwear that was still black as a Monday on Wall Street, but very fashion-forward. Ankle-hugging, ass-kicking boots from the Wicked Witch of the West collection with hyperextended toes terminating in anally intrusive points the size and shape of the Hope diamond. They were ludicrous-looking things, but a clear and promising sign of avuncular defiance. From the way Nina was eyeballing Wendy, she appeared as intent on taking names as teeing up booty.

Wendy, for her part, seemed a bit disappointed. Maybe she had imagined that Chinese secret agents and a Communist Party bigwig would come across like a pair of James Bonds and the villain-du-jour. But in their standard black suits and matching haircuts, the trio looked more like pallbearers for hire. Their disinterested expressions only added to the impression.

I assumed all the gloominess in the room meant that the secret agents had failed to dig up locally applicable dirt on Mickey Wu. Li Wei's lack of agitation also made me optimistic that Nina hadn't mentioned the Dimmu Borgir deal. Feeling sanguine and having a few minutes to spare, I decided to turn their frowns upside down.

"I know how you can nail Mickey Wu," I announced cheerfully.

All three perked up with a decidedly predatory air, as if I was a Friday afternoon walk-in reporting that my entire family had just died in a bus crash.

"How?" Li Wei demanded.

I tossed Barb's copy of the *Vancouver Sun* to Agent Wang. "That's Mickey Wu's boat."

While Li Wei pored over the newspaper article, I sidled up to Nina's desk. "Is the contract ready?" I asked her quietly.

She held out a manila envelope without taking her eyes off Wendy. "Who's your little friend?"

"My name's Wendy," Wendy said brightly. "I really wanted to thank you for helping get Dante and Richard back."

Nina's facial features began to thaw. "Are you a friend of theirs?"

Wendy nodded. "Dante and I are *very* close. And of course Richard is a total doll."

"Isn't he just? I totally freaked out when I heard what happened to them. And when Jake came to me for help..." Nina shrugged modestly. "But since he's too obtuse to properly introduce us, my name is..."

"Nina. I know." Wendy smiled radiantly. "You're the narcissistic ex-wife."

I tugged the manila envelope free from Nina's abruptly white-knuckled grip. Wendy hadn't exactly scored me any points just now, but scoring with Nina had been sliding further and further down my priority list lately.

"This is incredible," said Agent Chung.

Welcoming the distraction, I turned my attention back to them. Li Wei appeared to be salivating heavily as he finished reading the article. "I thought you guys would like it," I said. "And since the media is all over this thing, the cops will be chomping at the bit to nail someone for it. All you have to do is give them the corporate paperwork showing that Mickey Wu owns the company that owns that boat. Next stop, Deportationville."

"Unless he's already made a run for it. He left home with a suitcase yesterday," Agent Wang said. "A man of his wealth could be anywhere by now," he added dejectedly.

"Don't worry. He's still in town," I assured them.

"How do you know this?" Li Wei asked suspiciously.

At this point it became difficult not to look smug. "Because we're on our way to meet him right now."

What followed can only be described as a hubbub. To regain control of the room I was forced to explain the backstory, leaving out certain elements pertaining to rogue agents of the Chinese Ministry of Public Security and focusing instead on the heroic liberation of Richard and Dante. I was vague about what I would be trading for them, but Li Wei and the super spies weren't interested anyway. The drug bust gave them what they needed to nail Mickey Wu and now all that mattered was getting him into custody.

"We will come with you," Agent Wang said eagerly.

"No, you won't," I countered.

"We must," Agent Chung said. "From what you have told us, Wu will undoubtedly leave town immediately after your meeting today."

"Yeah, probably." I considered the situation for a moment. "Okay, no, you're right. He will, for sure. But you still can't come to the meeting."

Further hubbub ensued. Perhaps our recent shenanigans at Mickey Wu's place had earned me a modicum of trust or professional respect, because I was eventually able to reach a compromise with Agents Wang and Chung: They could come with us, but Wendy and I would go in alone to make the trade. As soon as we came out with Richard and Dante, they were free to charge in and grab Mickey Wu.

Once our friends were safe, I really couldn't have cared less what fate the machinery of multijurisdictional justice would eventually churn out for Mickey Wu—though I did hope that Li Wei would see to it that all of them were awarded whatever the Chinese Communist Party equivalent was to the Transport Canada Certificate of Bravery.

"I'm coming, too," Li Wei declared, possibly already envisioning the award ceremony.

The secret agents exchanged a look but neither spoke. It was clear to everyone in the room—including, I suspected, Li Wei himself—that he would be nothing more than a self-serving liability.

Generally, I preferred to let an awkward silence play itself out, but we had no time to spare. "Great idea. Let's go."

Chapter Fifty-two

Apparently, I still hadn't earned Li Wei's trust because he demanded that we head to the meeting convoy-style. I didn't protest. The last thing I wanted was to waste any more time debating operational logistics.

As soon as they disappeared around the corner to get their car, I texted Agent Wang the address and drove away.

"Far be it for me to question your meticulously improvised plan…" Wendy said.

"I appreciate that."

"But remember when I said you could use all the help you could get?"

"Sure. That's why I brought along my trusty ninja sidekick."

Wendy didn't return my grin. Maybe she just had her game-face on, but more likely it was nerves. Now that we were finally on our way to the meet, I was feeling a bit tense myself. All of a sudden, the gambits I had planned didn't seem nearly as foolproof as they did at half-past spliff the night before.

"So why didn't you let your spy buddies come with us into the meeting? Isn't it their job to deal with guys like Mickey Wu?"

"I suspect they tend to bag more bureaucrats than drug lords. But sure, I suppose you could say they have some broadly applicable experience."

"Unlike either of us," Wendy opined.

I held up a finger. "I disagree. I believe we have a far superior understanding of the drug-dealer mindset."

"It just seems like Mickey Wu would know the jig is up if we walk in with a couple of heavy-hitters from the Chinese Ministry of Public Security."

"Therein lies the problem," I said.

Wendy frowned. "Really? Because in my head it sounded more like the solution."

"Right now, I'm betting that Mickey Wu wants to do a quick, quiet trade so he can get the hell out of town before the cops figure out whose boat they have. But if we show up with the super spies in tow, he's liable to freak out."

"Because you ratted him out."

I winced. "Uncharitable phrasing, but yeah, I suspect he'll see it that way. And not just him. Mickey Wu set his daughter up with a cushy new life using the ill-gotten gains that the Chinese government wants back. This thing today is about Mickey trying to protect her from getting dragged down with him. So, if he thinks I've put them both in the crosshairs..."

"You're worried he might get nasty?"

I nodded.

"What about your Norwegian buddy?"

"I *know* he's going to get nasty when he discovers he's losing another business partner. Unless I have a chance to paint a bigger picture for him first." I turned onto French Street, pulled into a spot and turned off the ignition. "Shall we?"

I almost didn't recognize the place in the daylight, but a quick circumnavigation of the house next to 8551 French Street confirmed it. Mickey Wu was holed up at The Norwegian's soon-to-be-condominiums.

His neighbours showed more pride of ownership than he did, though I had no idea why. Most of the other houses on the block were "Vancouver Specials," a stigmatic style of building that proliferated through unloved parts of the city in the Seventies and Eighties. Brick-and-stucco boxes girded by incongruously ornate iron railings. A few daring architects added other brick-and-metal architectural flourishes to draw and punish the eye. I found myself wishing The Norwegian success with his property-development aspirations.

"Is this the place?" Wendy eyed the drawn and battered blinds of the grow-op house apprehensively.

A gust of wind cooled the sweat I hadn't noticed permeating the soft cotton of my mustard-coloured dress shirt. Like me, it had worn thin in places and didn't button all the way to the top. A chill scuttled across my back as I sniffed the warm, ganja-laced air being expelled into the atmosphere by an industrial blower fan that had been punched through the basement wall, half-hidden behind some recently planted, seldom-watered shrubbery. The purple, exfoliating house paint chafed my conscience, mostly as a citizen of Vancouver, but also a former grower who prided himself on running a tidy operation. I shook my head. "This one's where the after-party will be."

I kicked a moss-laden asphalt shingle back onto the lawn and led her next door to our destination that was equipped with identical drawn and battered blinds. The paint sloughing off this one was gun-metal grey. "Ready?" I knocked on the door without risking an answer.

A leather-clad barrel chest darkened the peek-a-boo window in the front door. We listened as numerous deadbolts were unlocked. The door swung inward with a creaking complaint that bespoke infrequent use or a strong aversion to maintenance.

As I stepped inside, I spotted the super spies' Chevy Impala turning onto the street.

The door was already closing again when Wendy slid in behind me, oblivious to the surprised scowl aimed down at her.

The entrance would have felt cramped without three people in it. Like angels dancing on the head of a pin, we shuffled awkwardly on parquet flooring scarred by arcane Norse rituals, both social and commercial, conducted in the dark at all hours of the day and night. A dusty bulb burned in a wall-sconce. I winked at my dim reflection in the wall of glass bricks to my right as stucco abraded my left shoulder. Wendy was wedged against me, warming my spleen.

For a moment, no one said anything. I couldn't. My breath had caught in my throat, refusing to be exhaled into the mix of stale beer, expensive cologne, and mildew that filled the air. From somewhere deeper in the house I could hear the braying of a discount furniture store ad on the radio.

The Norwegian seemed disinclined to relinquish the entry-way so I showed myself into the living room, where I found Mickey Wu sitting in one of the two lawn chairs in the room. His expression was equal parts fascism and pathos. The jaw muscles were getting a good workout but the intensity of Mickey's stare was undermined by the dark circles under his eyes. The blue blazer was gone and sweat stains had washed the starch out of his foundational white dress shirt.

A few feet behind him were Richard and Dante. I could only assume that the lack of home furnishings, rather than Scandinavian hospitality, explained why they were sitting on the floor, cable-locked to a pile of cinder blocks.

"Took you long enough, Constable." Richard offered up a pale imitation of his usual megawatt smile. His ever-present stubble had gone fallow, now verging on something beard-like. The Caesar hairstyle Richard employed to hide his slightly receding hairline lay limp and oily.

Dante's head hung low but I could see that the left side of his face was covered with a livid bruise.

Rage took hold of me. "Which one of you assholes did that to him?"

The Norwegian sneered. "He slipped getting out of the bath."

"You expect me to believe that?"

Richard put a protective arm around Dante's shoulders. "It's true, Jake. There isn't even a shower curtain in the bathroom. Water gets everywhere. It's very dangerous." His tone was admonishing.

Dante looked up at last. "Wendy!" he exclaimed. "Are you ever a sight for sore eyes. Please tell me you brought my MegaMan vitamins. They've fed us nothing but Domino's pizza—I may have to do a cleanse."

Mickey Wu groaned. "This one never shuts up about the food." He pointed at Wendy. "Who's the woman? I thought I told you to come alone."

"You did." They say it's better to beg forgiveness than ask permission. At the moment I wasn't interested in doing either. "I didn't."

Wendy saluted him. "Don't mind me, I'm just the sidekick."

"Enough talk," The Norwegian rumbled. "Give Mr. Wu his documents so we can be done with all this."

I feigned surprise. "You thought I was just going to walk in here with them? After what he tried to pull last time?"

Mickey Wu's eyes narrowed as Wendy's widened. "You didn't bring them?" they said in unison.

I had just enough time to shake my head before throwing my hands up to stop it from being slammed into the wall. I leaned there, bracing for a second attempt but none came.

"Bad time to be playing games." The Norwegian frisked me like a baker kneading dough. He lifted my jacket and yanked the manila envelope from out of the back of my pants. "Pathetic." He tossed it to Mickey Wu, who eagerly ripped it open.

His expression darkened as he scanned the first few pages. "What the hell is this?"

Chapter Fifty-three

Mickey waved the document at me angrily. "This is…" The double-take would have been comical if not for the stakes. "A sales and marketing agreement? You expect me to believe this is what was in the safety-deposit box? It has nothing to do with my daughter."

"Not your daughter, no. But it does concern you as a shareholder of Dimmu Borgir, Inc."

"What concerns me right now is what you have done with the information on my daughter," he snarled, throwing the document aside.

Dante recoiled as the papers exploded around him like sharp-edged butterflies before fluttering to the floor.

Mickey Wu hadn't taken the bait, but I wasn't really expecting him to. I was trolling for bigger fish. The Norwegian hesitated only briefly before gathering up the contract from the floor beside Mickey Wu's chair. "Blue Coast Realty—that's Nina's agency?"

I nodded.

Dante straightened up in a hurry. "You're getting her mixed up in all this?"

Richard let out a low whistle. "Looks like someone grew a pair while we've been away."

"You talked to Nina for me?" The Norwegian's tone had

softened noticeably. His rumbling voice sounded almost soothing, like a boulder rolling down a mossy hillside.

It was a step in the right direction. I was still on slippery terrain and could get crushed if I lost my footing. I cautiously advanced my position. "She was really intrigued by your condo idea."

"The Norwegian's going to build condos?" Richard whispered in amazement.

I didn't dispute the notion. "His company is called Dimmu Borgir. It means dark fortresses."

"Sounds very dramatic," Dante stage-whispered. "Sign me up for pre-sales."

"Who cares about the stupid condos?" Mickey Wu exclaimed, furious, but his partner was too engrossed in reading through the contract to notice.

"Blue Coast Realty LLP is seeking an exclusive sales and marketing arrangement in British Columbia and the People's Republic of China for all properties developed by or for Dimmu Borgir, Inc.", The Norwegian announced happily, his basso profundo drowning out Mickey Wu's increasingly shrill tenor.

"China?" The Norwegian repeated, his voice hushed with awe.

He held up the document with the same tender reverence with which a priest holds a bible. "This is amazing."

"Most of Nina's clientele is based there." I paused. "Weren't you telling me there's some serious money funneling out of China into Vancouver real estate these days?"

He nodded dreamily.

"It's actually Nina's uncle who drums up business at that end." I smacked my head. "I almost forgot to mention that he's a co-owner of Blue Coast Realty."

The Norwegian paused now and turned, frowning. "I don't like doing business with people I don't know."

"His name is Li Wei. Hey, you know he's actually in town right now…how about I introduce you guys?"

"He's a real estate agent back in China?"

"Real estate is more of a sideline." I brushed some errant flakes of early-eighties stucco off my shoulder. "His day job is Deputy Director of the Department of Infrastructure Development in the Chinese Commerce Federation." It had taken me ten minutes and two cups of coffee to memorize Li Wei's title that morning, so I took my time saying it. I sat back for a little while longer to let it sink in.

My arm went numb when The Norwegian hit me, an open-handed slap that sounded like a balloon popping. Or possibly my deltoid. "Good work, Constable. This is huge."

With my working arm I fished a pen out of my pocket and offered it to The Norwegian. "Should we seal the deal?"

Mickey Wu viciously kicked the lawn chair aside as he shot to his feet. "I don't want to hear one more word about that damned contract. Where the hell is the information on my daughter?"

"I told you already, it's not here."

"You've broken our deal," he spat. His hands closed into fists. "So now The Norwegian is going to break your legs. Then your friends' legs. Then bones of his choosing until you deliver what you promised."

Mickey glared at his partner expectantly. The Norwegian missed his cue, busy as he was signing the agreement.

I bounced on my toes, appreciating the continued use of my legs as I walked a tightrope between Mickey Wu and The Norwegian. "I don't think he heard you, Mickey. We're cutting deals right now. The good news is I'm prepared to offer you a new one as well."

He ignored me, his breathing rapid and noisy through flared nostrils, while he waited for The Norwegian to finish up the paperwork. "You're never going to have any condos to sell without my cash," Mickey sneered. "And if you ever want to see any of it, you'll force your friend here to give… me… the… information… on… my… daughter… right… *now*."

The Norwegian hesitated, his eyes pivoting back and forth between us. He emitted a sound halfway between a sigh and a growl. "Are you going to give him what he wants, Constable?"

"Eventually, if he behaves. The bigger question is can Mickey give you what you want?"

The Norwegian put his hands on his hips. "What do you mean?"

"How is Mickey coming up with the cash he promised you when all his dope is sitting in a VPD evidence room right now?"

The Norwegian frowned at Mickey Wu, who glared at me and snorted one hundred percent pure spite. The man had the nostrils of a Kentucky Derby winner.

"I was surprised when you guys abandoned ship so quickly that night—I don't care how rich you are, that boat was way too nice to ditch. It finally made sense when I saw in the paper that *The Chairman* had a few hundred kilos of opium on it."

Mickey Wu fluttered his hands in the air dismissively. "I can bring more in through different channels."

I crossed my arms and raised a hand to tap my pursed lips thoughtfully. "How can you do that if you're not here?"

When he didn't respond, I took the liberty of bringing The Norwegian up to speed myself. "The only reason he's still walking around a free man is because *The Chairman* is owned by one of Mickey's companies back in China. The cops haven't been able to trace it back to him yet."

The Norwegian didn't take his eyes off Mickey Wu the entire time I was speaking. His head was cocked like a Great Dane as he hung on my every word.

"You're not planning to skip out on me, are you?" he asked Mickey.

Recognizing the ominous disappointment in his voice, I experiencing a gut-clenching flashback to when I informed The Norwegian I would no longer be supplying him with Granddad's Ganja. I hated to draw his attention back to me right then, but I had more deals to close. "Mickey's got no choice. He won't be much good to you if he stays in town and gets nabbed by the cops."

Mickey Wu didn't speak or move. Even his nostrils had closed for business.

The Norwegian wheeled on me. "You're defending him now? We wouldn't have been sitting around on that stupid boat in the first place if it wasn't for you. What is it, a hobby for you to continually fuck up my business?"

His breath smelled of hamburger, heavy on the secret sauce. I held up a finger. "Technically, Granddad's Ganja was my business." When The Norwegian growled deep and low, I quickly moved on. "Don't forget that I just lined up a new partnership for you. If Mickey's leaving you short on capital, why not talk to Uncle Wei over at the Chinese Commerce Federation?"

I stopped talking when The Norwegian began shifting his weight from side to side. I recognized the body language. It was a precarious moment. The Norwegian's gaze slashed the air between Mickey Wu and me, weighing us up as he prepared to cut one of us down to size.

Mickey had a vacant, puzzled expression on his face, as if he was unable to grasp what was happening. A second later, he gave an involuntary shudder and his gaze came back into focus. Mickey opened his mouth to speak at the same moment The Norwegian sighed. The trenchcoat complained audibly as his shoulders dropped within it. The Norwegian gave me the nod. "When can you introduce us?"

I grinned at Wendy, my scalp tingling with sweat. "One down, one to go," I whispered to her, right before the super spies burst through the front door.

Chapter Fifty-four

Agents Wang and Chung picked a bad time to crash the party, but I didn't blame them. I saved that sentiment for the stuffed shirt behind them.

"Time's up, Constable," Li Wei hissed, elbowing through the increasingly crowded room. His eyes darted around the room and its occupants suspiciously.

"Who the hell are these guys?" thundered The Norwegian.

"We are from the Chinese Ministry of Public Security and we are here for that man." Agent Wang pointed at Mickey Wu. "This doesn't concern the rest of you," he added hastily, gawking up at The Norwegian.

Agent Chung was similarly distracted by the living manifestation of Dimmu Borgir. Li Wei couldn't see much of anything since he had scuttled back behind the agents after catching sight of The Norwegian. Dante stared at the three of them, dumbfounded by their arrival, while Wendy and I silently exchanged a "now what?" look.

Which was why none of us noticed the pistol in Mickey Wu's hand until Richard shouted, "Gun!"

Mickey Wu was trembling with rage as he waved the Glock around like a water diviner with sunstroke. First he aimed at the super spies, then me, then at Li Wei when he peeked out from behind Agent Chung. Finally he zeroed in on Richard and Dante when Li Wei ducked back.

A slow-motion dance ensued. Those of us not locked to cinder blocks began slowly edging away from Mickey Wu. When he noticed and brought the gun around, we froze and the previous target began to move.

Only Wendy and The Norwegian stood their ground. Probably because Mickey Wu had thus far exhibited sufficient good sense not to aim the gun anywhere near The Norwegian. Wendy had cleverly taken refuge in the safe harbour that was his leeward side. It's been said that no man is an island, but The Norwegian was about as close as they come.

"Wow, Jake, you totally called it," she whispered. "He's definitely freaking out."

Agent Wang raised his hands in a placating manner. "Put the gun down and let Mr. Constable and his friends go, Mr. Wu. Then we can talk about your situation."

His request was well intentioned, and I appreciated it, but it lacked the desired effect.

The Glock settled on a target. "This is your doing, Constable?" Mickey spat.

I kept my eyes on Mickey Wu but I could feel the weight of The Norwegian's incredulous glare on me as well. "*You* brought in the cops?"

Allegiances were crumbling rapidly. I defended myself as best I could. "Not cops. Secret agents. And the guy hiding behind them is your new business partner. Allow me to introduce you to Li Wei." I spread my hands in what I hoped was a cross-cultural gesture of camaraderie.

At the mention of his name, Li Wei's face popped back into view with an alarmed expression. His uncomprehending eyes locked on The Norwegian, who grinned and gave him a friendly wave.

"You've ruined my life!" Mickey's voice was shrill. His knuckles were white on the handle of the Glock as he waved his arms wildly in the air, in the grips of a full-blown tantrum.

A savage kick sent one of the lawn chairs spinning in my direction. "Do you even know what you've done? By giving these men the…"

"Address!" I yelped, cutting him off. "Yes, Mickey, I know— I led the Ministry right to you by giving them this address. And now you and *you alone* will have to deal with them." I tore my eyes from the pistol and made eye contact with Mickey, attempting to give him a meaningful look but hampered by the fact that I was on the verge of doing a little freaking out of my own. Mickey had clearly blown a fuse. He was done dealing in subtleties for the day. One of his eyes was twitching a Morse code message of pure hatred. From the back of his throat came the strange, staccato soundtrack of cognitive gears grinding.

His shoulders slumped and his hands dropped to his sides. Encouraged, I raised my hands and my eyebrows, hoping to amplify my telepathic message that I hadn't given them the documents on his daughter.

Mickey smiled at me. Then he raised the Glock.

Wendy's arm shot out with super ninja speed so I almost missed the little black stun gun in her hand as it darted beneath The Norwegian's leather coat. A split second later she was knocked off her feet, flying across the room as he erupted in a volcanic convulsion. The rest of us cringed as The Norwegian performed a berserker jig, howling as his limbs flailed spasmodically. An arm with the girth and weight of a well-fed anaconda shot out, taking Mickey Wu across the jaw.

Mickey dropped like a bag of wet cement. The Glock fired as he hit the ground.

I dove past The Norwegian, narrowly dodging a knee the size of a bowling ball, and piled onto Mickey Wu. I wedged a forearm up under his chin to cut off the airflow, just like Thaddeus had taught me. "Don't even think about moving," I growled.

"Uh, Jake, I think he's already unconscious," Richard whispered as the room grew quiet.

The Norwegian was bent over with his hands on his knees, his breathing coming hard and fast. "What the fuck, lady?" he groaned.

"Sorry, big fella," Wendy said as Agent Chung helped her to her feet. "Someone had to take Mickey Wu out before he shot Jake."

Li Wei lay on the floor, moaning as blood leaked out of a hole in the toe of one of his shiny black shoes.

Richard rattled his handcuffs. "Where are the keys?" His tone so agitated that even The Norwegian took notice. Dante quivered beside him, blinking rapidly. He looked ready to bolt for the door hauling the pile of cinder blocks behind him.

The Norwegian prodded Mickey Wu's inert form with a size-fourteen boot. "Check his pockets."

Having learned from past mistakes, I knew enough to start my search with the jacket. Nothing. Cursing the current svelte fashions yet again, I unceremoniously jammed my hands down into Mickey Wu's pants pockets and was rewarded with the keys, a black comb, and ninety dollars in cash. After a brief hesitation, I jammed the comb back into his pants.

"Lunch is on Mickey Wu," I announced. After everything he put us all through, I figured it was the least he could do.

The Norwegian blocked my way when I started toward Richard and Dante to unlock them. "Hold on, Constable. Where do you think you're going?"

I gave my friends an enquiring look. "The Elbow Room?"

They nodded. When The Norwegian didn't budge, I jangled the keys in my hand impatiently. "Preferably before the cops show up to find out if the 911 call about a shot being fired was for real."

He considered this for a moment before moving out of my way. "Everyone get the hell out of my house right now!"

"May we?" Agent Chung inquired timidly, pointing at Mickey Wu, still sprawled out cold in a puddle of his own drool.

"Go ahead," The Norwegian sighed. "He's no damn good to me now."

Agent Wang was tending to Li Wei so Agent Chung tried to drag Mickey Wu toward the door by himself.

After watching him sympathetically for a moment, Wendy stepped forward. "Can I help?"

Agent Chung gestured toward Mickey Wu's feet but Wendy shook her head and motioned for him to step back. When he had, she gave Mickey Wu a quick prod, causing him to briefly do the worm before sitting up and looking around in confusion. Wendy grinned and blew on the end of her stun gun before sliding it back into her pocket.

As she was helping Dante and Richard toward the door, I pulled Agent Wang aside. "Is Li Wei going to be okay?"

He nodded. "Two toes are gone, and the shoe is ruined. But he will be fine."

"At least he got his foot in the door with Operation Fox Hunt."

Agent Wang flashed me a wry smile.

"Or maybe he really put his foot in it this time." I handed Agent Wang the newly minted contract between Blue Coast Realty and Dimmu Borgir, Inc. "Can you give this to him when he's, you know…?"

"Back on his feet?"

I grinned. "You should read that contract over as well," I added as I walked out the door.

Chapter Fifty-five

The following night, all my troubles seemed a world away. I lounged on a rooftop deck with Richard and Dante, admiring the warp and glow of the city lights reflecting off the waters of English Bay.

"This is more like it," Dante sighed, sipping his mojito. The bruise on his face had already dulled to a subtle mocha that blended nicely with his permatan, and I was pretty sure he was wearing a new shirt.

"Yeah, thanks for having us over, Jake." Richard rubbed his clean-shaven jaw with satisfaction.

I waved away the gratitude. "Least I could do after making you guys put up with The Norwegian's hospitality."

"True," said Richard.

"Hold on now, that wasn't entirely Jake's fault," Dante said.

"Also true," Richard agreed. "I told you not to make fun of The Norwegian's coat but did you listen?"

Dante shrugged helplessly. "Have you taken a good look at that thing?"

"Still," Richard chided, turning to me. "But you finally managed to make your peace with that beast, right? He's not mad at us anymore?"

"I hope not."

Vinyl creaked as Richard sat upright in his chaise lounge.

"What does that mean? I thought you made all his wildest real estate dreams come true when you hooked him up with Nina's uncle."

"I did."

"So what happened?"

"I got Li Wei arrested." Distant sirens disturbed the silence that followed.

"You got Nina's uncle arrested?" Dante asked at last, possibly with a hint of admiration in his voice.

"Yup."

Richard put his drink down carefully. "For what?"

"Economic corruption."

Dante snorted. "Is there any other kind?"

"Corruption of the flesh. Corruption of minors. Police corruption. Political corruption," Richard recited, his face illuminated by the glow of his phone.

"I didn't even know economic corruption was a crime," Dante continued, cutting Richard off. "I thought it was just called doing business."

"Rrrowrr," Richard whispered to him.

I grinned, swirling the ice around in my glass. "The Chinese government begs to differ."

Richard gaped. "The Chinese government?"

I nodded.

"You got him arrested in *China?*" Now there was no question about it. Dante's tone was infused with admiration.

"I believe Agents Wang and Chung may have taken him into custody while he was still enjoying the amenities of China Airlines' first-class cabin. But, yes, he'll be facing charges back home. Along with his newly minted business partner, Mickey Wu." I paused, mostly for effect. "Because of him, actually."

Richard closed his eyes and raised his hands like a mime trapped in a box. "Back the tuk-tuk up a minute. I thought Li Wei came over here for the express purpose of getting Mickey Wu arrested. Since when were they partners?"

"Since The Norwegian signed that contract I gave him while I was saving your asses. He and Nina entered into it on behalf of their companies, Blue Coast Realty and Dimmu Borgir, Inc. Which Li Wei and Mickey Wu are co-owners of, respectively." I struggled unsuccessfully to suppress an errant grin.

"So Nina used to be partnered up with her very wealthy, totally connected uncle?" Dante asked.

I nodded.

"But now, thanks to you, Li Wei has been arrested for colluding with a thong salesman?" Richard asked.

I held up a finger. "And opium-smuggler. Yes."

"And her new partner, again thanks to you, is a Norwegian berserker, whose only known business connections are said thong salesman, and, well…you?" Richard's face radiated awe. And pride. I basked in it before correcting him.

"The Norwegian assures me he's not a berserker anymore. Just a property-developer."

Dante raised a finger of his own. "In a positively *medieval* leather trench coat."

"How does Nina feel about you getting her uncle arrested?" Richard asked cautiously.

"She's pretty mad."

"Forget Nina," said Dante. "How does The Norwegian feel about it? Wasn't Li Wei a major sweetener in the contract with Nina's agency?"

"Yeah, I don't think he's too happy about it, either. But the deal still stands, and Nina's not going anywhere. She's a Canadian citizen, so Operation Fox Hunt is no threat to her." I shrugged. "Nina may not have all Li Wei's connections back in China, but she's still a top realtor in this town with a big-money clientele."

Dante shook his head slowly, his lips pursed thoughtfully. "Nina and The Norwegian, wow. Do you think they will work out?"

I paused, not having thought about all that until this moment. "They're both intelligent, ambitious people with shared passions for real estate and sales and marketing. Who knows? Maybe they'll end up making beautiful condos together."

Dante's phone chirped. He read the incoming text and stood up. "Wendy's downstairs. I'll go let her in."

"So," Richard said after Dante left.

"So?"

"I guess that'll finally be it for you and Nina."

I consulted my glass of bourbon for a moment. "It was over a long time ago."

Richard reached over and squeezed my forearm. "Duh."

We sat in silence until Dante returned with Wendy in tow. I was surprised to see that she had arrived alone. "Where's Barb? You told her she was invited, didn't you? Only as your '+1' of course, but she should be here, since she did play a minor role in our rescue mission."

Wendy gave me a disappointingly eager smile. "She'll be here soon."

I nodded without enthusiasm.

"She just had to pick up her date," she added.

My mouth hung open, waiting patiently for my brain to come up with the proper response. "Date?"

Wendy nodded slowly, her face betraying no emotion.

"And you're…okay with that?"

She continued to nod slowly. "I really am."

I did a visual check on Richard and Dante to see if this was making sense to them, but they were busy examining each other's cuticles.

Wendy broke the silence. "So are you going to offer a lady a drink?"

By the time I returned with another mojito, Dante had Wendy over his shoulder, growling with mock ferocity as he threatened retribution because she had swatted his precisely styled man-bun askew.

"Aren't you going to defend her from my brutish squeeze?" Richard teased as he helped himself to Wendy's mojito.

"Since when does the master need protection from her student?" I retorted.

Dante chortled. "Master? Wendy? I taught her everything she knows about Tae Bo, and Tae Bo is life! I am the master!"

Wendy squealed as he spun around with her, digging his fingers into her ribs.

I dropped back into my chair. "You going to take that from him? Come on, Wendy, show us your ninja moves."

"Ooooh, sounds scary." Dante put Wendy down and started dancing around her, randomly freezing in poses, some borrowed from Ralph Macchio, others from Madonna.

I felt retroactively relieved that I brought Wendy to rescue Dante, and not the other way around. "Is that all she taught you?"

"You can't teach this kind of stuff, Constable. It comes from within," Dante replied before dropping into Richard's lap.

Wendy avoided my eye as she drained her mojito. "Great view from up here."

I glanced back at Dante. "Seriously, though. Didn't Wendy teach you jujutsu? Isn't that how you two met?"

Dante looked puzzled but Richard burst out laughing. "Jujutsu? These two creampuffs? As if!"

Dante pinched Richard. "I'm plenty tough, bitch!" He smiled patronizingly at me. "But I'm no ninja, Jake. Sorry to put a crimp in your fantasy life. Wendy and I met when we were both working in the nutritional supplements department of Whole Foods."

"Wendy, what the…?" I looked over just as her phone began moaning the first few saxophone notes from Tom Waits' "Way Down in the Hole."

She held up a finger and answered the call. "Barb's here," she announced. "I'll go let her in." Wendy turned, knocking over a deck chair as she darted back into the condo.

"So you've got a thing for ninjas." Dante grinned as he climbed off of Richard and picked up the chair. "I never would've guessed."

Rather than answer him, I allowed myself to wallow in self-pity as yet another childhood fantasy turned to dust. Time to start shopping for a new sidekick.

Richard disappeared into the condo and returned with the bottle of Woodford Reserve. "Freshen your drink?" He filled my glass to the brim without waiting for an answer.

"Uh, thanks."

Richard clinked his glass off of mine. "Bottoms up."

I raised the glass to my mouth but most of it ended up on my lap when I heard Barb's date say, "Hello, son."

Chapter Fifty-six

The rest of the evening wasn't what I had envisioned, but it wasn't bad. A frazzled mental inventory of my reaction to finding out that my mom was with Barb revealed that what I worried might be disapproval was really surprise sharpened by the embarrassment of being the last to know. The real shocker for me was that Captain Constable would flout the Coast Guard's human resources policy by pursuing a romance with one of her subordinates.

After a couple more drinks, though, I started to understand why. They were good together, bonded in ways I could never fathom, possibly by a shared respect for the sea and Captain Constable. As father figures went, I could probably do a lot worse.

Having my mom crash the party as Barb's date did still crank up the weird factor. The most awkward moment wasn't when I came upon them making out in the kitchen, though that was an early frontrunner. It was when the three of us were sitting together and my mom asked me to roll them a spliff.

"What's the matter, Jake?" she asked.

"Well, it's just that…Since when did you…?"

"Spit it out. What? Since when have I been gay?"

I shook my head. That, too, came as a surprise. But my mother's sexual inclinations ranked way down at the bottom of things I wanted to know about. "Since when did you smoke pot? I thought you were totally anti-drugs."

She chuckled. "Don't believe everything you read in the newspaper. Not that I don't enjoy taking down the occasional drug-smuggler with my best gal by my side." She smiled at Barb warmly.

Standing a little ways off, but evidently within earshot, Dante made a discrete gagging motion.

"Not that whole opium thing. I'm talking about my, uh... business."

"House-sitting? Not the career I would've chosen for you, but it's your life."

"No, I mean growing."

"What, like as a person? Please don't tell me you're going all West Coast spiritual on me. I just couldn't deal with it if you became a life coach."

Barb smirked. "Those who can, do. Those who can't, teach."

"Are you two being deliberately obtuse or does it just leak out of the uniforms? I am talking about the fact that I grew weed."

My mom regarded me with a bland expression, so I tried again. "As in pot? Ganja? *Marijuana.* The stuff I grew over at Granddad's place on Hornby Island? You do recall bumping into me just off the island one night a while back, don't you?"

"I'm not senile, Jake. Of course I remember fishing your butt out of the water. But if I didn't care that my dad grew weed there, why would I care if my son did?"

I shook my head, peering closely at her as I wondered whether she doth protest too much about the whole senility thing. "Granddad grew heirloom tomatoes."

"Sure, as a cover." She smiled nostalgically. "And, okay, yes, they turned out to be very good. But it would've been pretty hard to raise a family on what he brought home from the Gulf Islands farmer's markets. And nowhere near enough to buy himself a Greavette."

Barb inhaled sharply. "You never told me your family had a Greavette. Which one?"

"The Streamliner."

"Oh, my God, those are works of art." Barb's voice filled with awe.

"Don't remind me," my mom said bitterly.

"Sorry to interrupt, but what's a Greavette?" I asked.

My mom wouldn't meet my eye, but Barb more than made up for it by staring at me in amazement. "How is it possible that Captain Constable's son doesn't know what a Greavette is?"

"What can I tell you, the world is full of wonders," I replied impatiently.

Barb glanced at my mom, who for some reason seemed disinclined to jump into the conversation. "Greavettes are the most gorgeous hand-crafted, mahogany-hulled motorboats ever made. They're real collector's items. You're very lucky to own one." Before turning back to my mom, Barb hit me with her first full-strength, genuine smile, and I had to admit it wasn't without its charm. "You absolutely have to show it to me sometime."

My mom groaned. "I can't. This numbskull sank it." She delivered the words as if each one weighed a thousand pounds, every ounce of it unforgivable disappointment.

"I did? When…" The tumblers clicked. "Wait a minute, you're not talking about that mouldy old hulk of Granddad's I was driving the night I ran aground, are you?"

My mom's head dipped in what I took to be confirmation. A vein throbbed in her temple.

The silent treatment I was receiving let me hear the penny drop. "Hold on, is *that* what you've been so mad about? Why you've barely spoken to me since that night I ran aground? Because I sank an old boat?"

"It was a classic. I was going to restore it when I retired," my mom whispered.

I was dumbfounded. I stared at her for a moment, drawing a blank on what to say. Eventually, something occurred to me. "Sorry, mom," I whispered back.

● ● ● ● ● ●

Not long after that, Richard and Dante departed, pleading a post-traumatic Domino's pizza hangover. Barb and my mom followed them out after I promised to attend her award ceremony, and to come over for dinner on Sunday. Both Barb's suggestions, to which my mom and I grudgingly acquiesced.

I was surprised when Wendy defied the exodus. After getting us both another drink, I joined her back on the deck.

"So," she said.

"So." I smiled.

"Barb and your mom."

After surrendering my smile to Wendy, I nodded uncertainly. "Can't say as I saw that one coming."

Wendy gave me a searching look. "But you're okay with it?"

I hesitated, trying to find the right words. "I'm trying to be, it's just that..."

"You don't like Barb, do you?" She looked disappointed.

"I didn't," I admitted. "At first. But I'm starting to warm up to her."

"Then what is it?"

Before I answered, I softened my lip up with a good chewing. Just in case I needed it later on. "The age difference," I said at last.

Wendy stared at me for a moment before rendering judgment. "Pathetic."

"How would you like it if *your* mom was a cradle-robber?"

"Come on, it's not that bad. Barb's thirty-eight years old, the same age as me."

I studied her suspiciously. "Are you serious?"

Wendy nodded. "Mmm-hmm. And I advise you to choose your next words carefully, Constable."

I had none to offer, gripped by profoundly mixed emotions. I was relieved that the age spread between my mom and Barb wasn't so bad after all. Not embarrassingly bad, at least. Finding out that I was actually two years younger than Wendy suddenly made me feel about a decade older. I groaned slightly as I shifted uncomfortably on aching knees. "I think I need to sit down."

Wendy pulled over a couple of chaise lounges for us.

"Is it the yoga?" I asked, once I was comfortably sprawled.

"Is what the yoga?"

"How you stay so youthful?"

Wendy rolled her eyes. "Such a charmer."

"I'm serious."

She studied me for few seconds. "I guess I believe you. But yoga has nothing to do with it. I don't go in for that hippy-dippy stuff."

"But all that Lululemon stuff you wear—didn't you say it was for work?"

"It is. For my job as a vitamin rep. Show up in jeans and good luck selling a bottle, show up in stretchy pants and you'll sell twenty cases." Wendy looked over at me. "Well, maybe not you. But you get the idea."

I nodded happily. Yoga was off the list for both of us.

● • ● ● •

After a few minutes of sitting quietly beside Wendy, listening to the soft drone of traffic on the streets far below, I gradually became aware of another faint humming sound. As if every cell in my body had resumed the chorus they had been singing the night I met Wendy. Either that, or I was shivering from the damp chill of the West Coast night. Either way, moving a bit closer to Wendy seemed like a good idea.

"I'm getting cold." She abruptly stood up. Silence reigned as all the cells in my body went mute with disappointment. Until she spoke again. "Does that hot tub work?"

I had forgotten it was even there, so neither of us had our swimsuits with us. Soon enough, we forgot about them as well. The jets were on low, not so powerful that they would bruise the kidneys, but enough to create a full-body buzz.

Unless Wendy's kiss had done that. I couldn't say when or how it started. It just suddenly was. Everything, all-consuming. I also couldn't imagine it ending so much as expanding and evolving into something greater. Until it did end.

Wendy pulled back. "You're sure this is okay?"

I smiled. "Better than." I leaned in toward her.

"Not that. I mean us being here, in the tub."

I pulled back. "Oh, yeah. No need to worry," I assured her. "The owner isn't due back for another week."

To see more Poisoned Pen Press titles:

Visit our website:
poisonedpenpress.com
Request a digital catalog:
info@poisonedpenpress.com